MIRACLE OF THE Christmas Star

MIRACLE OF THE
Christmas Star

SUSAN DEAN ELZEY

SWEETWATER BOOKS
SPRINGVILLE, UTAH

ISBN 13: 978-1-59955-862-2

Published by Sweetwater Books, an imprint of Cedar Fort, Inc., 2373 W. 700 S., Springville, UT 84663
Distributed by Cedar Fort, Inc., www.cedarfort.com

LIBRARY OF CONGRESS CATALOGING-IN-PUBLICATION DATA

Elzey, Susan Dean, author.
  Miracle of the Christmas star / Susan Dean Elzey.
     pages cm
  Summary: Born with the cord wrapped around her neck, Hannah is pronounced
dead. A new star suddenly appears, shines directly on the baby, and she
revives. Hannah, however, does not grow up like the other children in
ancient Palestine: she must live her life unable to walk or talk.
  ISBN 978-1-59955-862-2
  1. Children with disabilities--Fiction. 2. Christmas stories. I. Title.

  PS3605.L92M57 2011
  813'.6--dc22

                                      2011012632

Cover design by Danie Romrell
Cover design © 2011 by Lyle Mortimer
Edited and typeset by Heidi Doxey

Printed in the United States of America

10 9 8 7 6 5 4 3 2 1

Printed on acid-free paper

To Mother and Daddy,
who have always loved me and helped me

1

A Star of Life

The night Sariah's baby of miracles, baby of sorrows, was born, a new star appeared in the velvet sky over their tiny village close to Bethlehem in Judah. It started as brightness and then gradually grew to brilliance until, just as Sariah gave one final scream that ended her agony, it streamed through the window over the bed, filling the room with warm light.

"God help us," Sariah's Aunt Mariam, who was attending her, shrieked. "The stars are falling from the sky."

She reached across and pushed the shutter closed, but it wouldn't latch and sprang back open as if it were alive. The stream of light could not be denied and shone around the low bed, dancing on the bedclothes that lay in a tangle at the foot.

Sariah called out, and Mariam's attention was turned back to the baby girl, who now lay lifeless and blue-faced between her mother's thighs, the cord wrapped tightly around her neck.

"My baby, my baby," Sariah whimpered, struggling to sit up to see why her baby was not crying.

"God help us," Mariam repeated, grabbing up the baby and cutting the cord with one quick pass of a knife that forever separated the life of the baby from the life of her mother.

"Breathe, child, breathe." Mariam unwound the cord and deftly tied it off, pulling the last away and flinging it down. She had no trouble seeing what she was doing since the brightness of the light seemed to increase with each passing moment. Noon that day had not been brighter than the light in the room as she shook the baby girl, who refused to respond.

Turning the baby upside down, Mariam pounded on her back, but still the baby's lifeless arms flopped, the blueness of her face spreading down to her soft limbs.

"My baby, give her to me," Sariah implored, her arms stretched out to take the infant.

But Mariam ignored the pleas of the new mother. She turned the baby over, shaking her again in a futile attempt to wake her, then turned her back to continue pounding her.

Minutes passed as she tried to force life into the baby. The room, awash in the light, was still—Sariah's soft cries the only sound. Finally, Mariam gathered the baby girl in her arms and wrapped her loosely in the cloth that had been prepared to swaddle a delicate newborn. She laid her without speaking on Sariah's chest that sucked in and out with her sobs.

"My baby, my baby," Sariah repeated, rubbing the baby's back, pleading for her to breathe.

Suddenly the light spread, illuminating every corner of the room and then the whole first floor of the tiny home. It crept up, bathing the mother and child in its soft brightness, reaching for the baby. Sariah raised one arm up to shield her eyes as Mariam pulled her scarf over her face, muttering once more, "God be with us, God be with us."

But the light softly whispered peace throughout the room. Sariah lowered her arm and watched as the light in the corners now gathered itself to the baby, who was lying still on Sariah's stomach.

Sariah felt the light's warmth, as if it were the sun, not a star, that touched her, seeking her child. She removed her hand from her baby's back and let the starlight dance then rest upon the baby. The blanket fell aside.

The blue flesh gradually turned to pink. An arm, then a leg moved slowly, melting, stretching into movement under the star's touch. One tiny second before the soft mouth gave a faint cry, the baby's wide, dark eyes opened, then squinted at the light.

Sariah reached for her child, and the light gave way. She pulled the baby up to hold her against her cheek and whispered into her ear.

"I will call you Hannah, for you live by the grace of God," she said. "Praise God."

Holding her gently breathing baby to her breast, Sariah lay back and rested.

2

From Miracle to Heartache

"She does not live by the grace of God, but by his curse," Mariam said to the young mother several months later. It wasn't the first time she'd spoken such words. Taking a break from sweeping out the small stone house where Sariah lived with her husband, Joshua, and Hannah, Mariam leaned on her broomstick and scowled as Sariah bent to the task of feeding the baby on her lap. Mariam was a large woman with a squarish face that tended to a scowl. Her eyebrows seemed permanently drawn together in disapproval, especially when she looked on her niece.

"Don't say that, Aunt Mariam. It will be all right." Sariah said, stopping her task of spooning milk into the baby's mouth. She sat at one of the crude stools surrounding the low table at the center of the room. A fireplace was at one end, and thick mats where they slept at the other. She hugged the baby to her as the child loudly sucked at the milk on her lips, thrusting her tongue out, as if to seek more.

Sariah called on her patience once more as Mariam's words cut into her heart, which stubbornly clung to the hope that all would be well. Her mind, however, had been forced to acknowledge her baby wasn't well. Hannah was not like Jared, the baby of her friend Joanna. Jared played on the floor several houses down, exploring his hands and feet and cooing in happiness.

Hannah's hands were clenched in tight fists against her thin chest. Her body was stiff and unyielding to the caresses of her mother and father. Her legs crossed when Sariah held her up to feel the sunlight upon her face or hear the song of the birds, even as her bright little smile lifted them from worry, if only for a moment at a time.

Worst of all, Hannah hadn't been able to nurse, biting, then sticking out her tongue, as if she didn't know what to do with the breast so lovingly offered to her. Instead, Sariah laboriously trickled milk from a spoon into her hungry baby's mouth.

"It would be better if that wondrous star, as you call it, had never shined through that window," Mariam said with a snort as she returned to her sweeping.

Sariah had lived with Mariam after her own mother died when she was eight, so Sariah knew her aunt's acid tongue and had often steeled herself against its slice. Now Mariam was a widow of two years, her grief at the loss of her husband not softening her but sharpening her with bitterness.

Each morning, out of a sense of duty and curiosity, she came to help Sariah, taking news back to her gossipy neighbors of how the child was doing, accepting the pity of the women as she told of her family's struggle and magnified her role in the events of the night the star shone over the countryside.

"What did our family do to deserve the wrath of God?"

she would wail tearlessly as her friends patted her back and clucked their tongues.

In the last few weeks, Sariah had struggled to remain strong under the relentless flood of Mariam's words, which often raged until the young mother's tears spilled over and down her cheeks. Sariah missed her own mother. Even though Sariah's memories of her were few, she knew if her mother were still alive, loving arms would comfort her and willingly reach out to lift the burden of her child from Sariah. She closed her eyes and tried to remember how her mother felt and smelled when, as a young child, Sariah ran to her and found herself wrapped in her arms. At times, she wondered if she really remembered what few memories she had or if they had been born of a desire through the years to know her mother's love. She wanted now to give that love to her child.

Yet the pain in her heart grew each minute of each day, even as her faith fought to survive and remind her of the warmth of the star that had made her baby breathe. Some said that angels had appeared to shepherds on the nearby hillsides that night, filling the sky with glorious singing and proclaiming the birth of their long-awaited savior.

But Sariah knew it was not her child the angels sang of, for the light had come, delivered its miracle, and left in its wake difficulty that at times came close to despair.

Sariah's warm tears dripped down onto her baby's face, one of them coursing down and filling a tiny eye. Startled, the baby blinked and looked up at her. She stopped her search for milk and for, just a moment, Sariah thought, Hannah caught a glimpse of her mother's heartache and reached her hand up.

The young mother smiled down at her baby, a pretty child who had inherited her mother's fine features, clear skin, and long eyelashes that framed her soft, dark eyes. Although

Hannah's hair was just beginning to curl around her ears, it was the same shade of brown as her mother's but touched with highlights of honey.

The joy of Hannah's acceptance numbed Sariah's sorrow, if only briefly. She never doubted that her baby had been restored to life by God, and that God in his infinite wisdom and goodness had purpose in placing this baby into her care.

"I love you," she whispered quietly so Mariam couldn't hear her. "You are my gift from God."

Thankfully, Mariam soon picked up a basket of clothes to mend and headed down the dusty street to her home. There she would find plenty of women who would shake their heads and agree with her on the utter futility of loving a child whose future could be that of the beggars in the street, crawling and clawing at the people who passed by, asking for a crumb of bread or a coin, never expecting a kind word from those who hurried by on strong, straight legs. Although their village was small and cripples few, Sariah remembered from her childhood one man with lifeless legs and slurred, wet speech who would sit at the corner of the village square and call to everyone to have mercy on him. Sariah always crossed the street upon seeing him.

That thought was too painful for Sariah to bear, so she pushed it deep within her. There were years ahead for her baby to learn and grow, and surely Sariah's love would complete the healing that heaven had started.

The cup of milk now gone, Hannah sighed with fulness as her eyes closed in fatigue.

"Sleep, my baby, sleep," Sariah said. She laid her gently down on the plump pallet on the floor and surrounded her with blankets so that her body, stiff while awake but looser in sleep, would touch only softness in slumber.

Hannah jerked as Sariah withdrew her arms but quickly succumbed.

A noise at the door made Sariah turn around and press her finger to her lips to warn her husband of the sleeping baby.

"I missed her," Joshua said, stooping to enter the low door. "I came as soon as I could, hoping to see her before she slept, but Elias broke a tool I needed to fix."

He kissed his young wife on the lips.

"Was she all right this morning?" he asked anxiously. "Did she eat?"

"She did," Sariah said, holding up the empty cup. "A whole cupful."

"Good," he said, but he held Sariah by both arms out in front of him and gazed into her eyes. "But you are sad."

She smiled, knowing she couldn't mask the pain in her eyes from her husband. He had the ability to dip into her soul. "Mariam . . ." she began.

He grunted in disgust.

"Mariam knows nothing," he said, folding Sariah in an embrace. "I will tell her she can't come anymore if she will not leave you alone."

"No," Sariah said. "I need help. I am sure difficult days lie ahead. The baby can be so fussy." She sighed from the depths of his strong arms. "If Mariam could just believe all will be well . . ."

"No one can match your faith, my beautiful one," he said. He tipped up her face and planted a quick kiss on her nose. Sariah smiled at his attention.

"Let's eat," he said. "You need some strength for the day ahead."

Well-liked by all in the village, Joshua was full of integrity and kindness. With high cheekbones and an olive complexion, he was handsome and strong from his strenuous job. His dark, curly hair defied control and accentuated dark eyes that often twinkled with a ready laugh. He was an apprentice with the aging blacksmith, Aaron, at the edge of the village, fixing the broken wagons and tools of the villagers and visitors who came through on the way to Jerusalem, a half-day's journey away. Aaron had promised Joshua that the business would be his when Aaron's hands became too stiff to fashion the iron into useful tools.

Living down the street from Sariah's family since he was young, Joshua had told Sariah he had watched her from the time she was a child, laughing under the care of her loving mother and then turning more solemn as her mother became sick and died. When she went to live with her aunt and her smiles became fewer, Joshua, six years older, had determined to return the smile to Sariah's lips when the time was right. No other girls, however hard they would try, got even a passing glance from Joshua. He watched and he waited, and when Sariah had turned sixteen, just two years ago, he had declared his love to her and promised if she would love him, he would always adore her as he had for years. It took no convincing, for she had also felt the love between them.

Sariah moved from her aunt and uncle's home a few streets over to a smaller house much like the others on this narrow street. By a cruel twist of fate, Joshua believed, Sariah's uncle had died soon after the marriage, leaving Mariam to be watched over. But the good man that he was, Joshua accepted his responsibility and had tried to do his duty by her. He wasn't as patient with her as Sariah was, however. One day when the time was right and he knew Sariah could manage on her own, he would tell Mariam she was not welcome in his home if she could not be kind to his young wife.

That would certainly keep her away, for it would be easier to stop the sun in its course than change Mariam's heart to kindness, Joshua thought with a chuckle as he filled his wife's plate before filling his own.

3

A Night of Weeping

The night that weeping was heard throughout Judah was warm, so warm that seven-month-old Hannah, who had been feverish throughout the day, was inconsolable. Sariah stood at the door for hours holding her and singing to her, while hoping for a cool breeze to calm her child. Other children Hannah's age had learned to crawl and stand, their tiny hands reaching out for crusts of bread and toys. But Hannah was unable to even hold her head up and open her hands, however often Sariah stroked them and stretched Hannah's little fingers out. Hannah's head lolled against her shoulder, even when she struggled to hold it up to see the sights around her. Each morning for Sariah began with a hope that her baby would be better that day, and each evening was marked by a sadness that she wasn't.

When Joshua returned from his work that day, Sariah had laid the fretful baby down on her bed and was bathing her with a wet cloth as she tried to coax her to take a little milk. Hannah squirmed and fussed under her mother's ministrations, her clenched fists hitting at some unseen annoyance and her wide eyes hot. Moist, dark curls clung to her forehead.

"What's wrong with her?" Joshua asked, standing over his wife and child with his brow furrowed.

"I think she is getting teeth, and the heat has been hard for her. She has eaten very little."

Joshua put his hands on his wife's shoulders and tried to massage the tightness from them.

"Let me care for her for a while, and when we have eaten, we'll go into the hillside where it is cooler," he said. "She'll like the fresh air, and it will do you good to walk under the stars."

Sariah sighed. "I'm fine. It is Hannah who worries me."

Joshua drew Sariah up with his strong hands under her elbows, embracing her from behind. For a moment, Hannah ceased her whimpering and looked up at her parents, curiosity on her face.

"See, she likes that idea," he said. "I know—fix us a simple meal to take, and we'll eat in the hills. It's been a long time since you've been away from the house."

He knelt beside the bed and picked up the bowl of milk, smiling down at his daughter.

"Will you eat for your father?" he asked her. She smiled up at him. A sound of contentment escaped her small mouth. "There, now. Take this milk, and we'll go sit under the stars that have blessed you."

As twilight descended, Joshua and Sariah made their way up a small hill where they could look down upon the village. Joshua carried Hannah over his shoulder, bracing her head that was not strong enough to hold itself straight. Sariah walked beside him, a basket of bread, cheese, and figs on her arm. Her heart felt lighter away from the village.

"Hear the sheep on the farther hill?" Joshua asked his daughter, holding her back and looking into her eyes. "Some say the night you were born, angels came to the shepherds and told them good news was at hand."

"Do you believe it, Joshua?" Sariah asked. She looked up at her husband with hope in her eyes.

"I do. I have heard from shepherds I trust that they were led to a small stable where a baby had been born. Surely, he is the one Israel has waited for."

"Oh, I hope so."

Joshua spoke with faith. "I don't know how, but all will be better when the savior comes."

Sariah looked up at him hopefully. "Do you think the savior could help Hannah?

"Perhaps." He shrugged his shoulders.

Suddenly, Sariah's mood changed. Her fears for Hannah, never far away, came crashing down upon her.

"What will we do if she cannot walk? How will we carry her? Holding her for so long this afternoon tired my arms already, and she is still tiny."

Sariah stumbled on a rock, and Joshua reached out with his arm to steady her.

"We will find a way," he answered confidently. He stopped at a large rock and looked down on the village. "Let's eat here. We can watch them, but they can't see us."

"It's nice to be away from prying eyes," Sariah said. She put down her basket and accepted the baby from Joshua. Then he spread out his cloak as a bed for Hannah. Taking her back, he gently laid her down.

A cool breeze teased her soft curls. She twisted and turned, looking back and forth from the dusky sky to her parents.

"Come, sit by me," Joshua said, leaning up against the rock and patting the ground beside him. "The baby is happy, and I am hungry."

"Me too," Sariah said. "I can't remember if I ate today."

Joshua frowned as he accepted food from her hand.

"You must take care of yourself, Sariah. Life without you beside me would not be life at all."

"I'll be fine." She stuffed a big piece of bread in her mouth, causing him to laugh once again, as they had done so readily in the days before Hannah was born.

"See. I'll be fine," she said with her mouth full and words muffled.

At the sound of their laughter, Hannah squealed and raised her thin arms to the sky.

Later, they sat in peace against the rock, Joshua's arms around Sariah, under the sky turned into night. Hannah had fallen asleep comfortably beside them, her forehead now cool to Sariah's touch.

"I don't want to go home," Sariah said with a contented sigh, snuggling back into Joshua.

"I don't think my back can stand a night's sleep against a rock," he said.

The village below had turned dark. Only a few candles could be seen flickering through the windows as people settled in for the night. A few shouts between the houses died out. In a rare moment, the quiet that the couple looked down upon settled into their hearts. Joshua had brought a small lantern, but the moon was so bright that he had extinguished it.

The sounds of the sheep on a neighboring hill seemed far away. The night was so still that Sariah could hear Joshua's heart beating against her cheek.

Gradually, though, the sound of galloping horses could be heard, shattering the quiet of the night. The thundering forced itself upon the couple's tranquility as they sat on the hillside. Sariah heard the noise first and sat up, trying to decide what it was. With her weight off him, Joshua stretched. When she realized it was horses, Sariah grabbed Joshua's leg. Their humble village seldom heard horses, and it usually meant soldiers were thundering through.

She looked down on the scene as her husband stood up, then quickly crouched. Coming down the road at a murderous pace was a group of perhaps twenty soldiers, carrying torches. Sariah's heart beat rapidly in fear as it always did at the sight of the cruel soldiers, whose stories were whispered about behind closed doors.

The couple watched as the horses sped into the village, the soldiers dismounting at the first house. They heard shouting, then screams and wails of children, of women, of men. Sariah's blood turned cold and her knees weak.

"Quickly, behind the rock," Joshua said, grabbing up the baby.

"What are they doing?" Sariah asked, too stunned to move.

"I don't know, but it can't be good," he answered, rising quickly. "Sariah, get behind the rock. Now."

She gathered up the remnants of their meal and stuffed it back into the basket. Joshua laid Hannah behind the rock and came back, grabbing his wife by the arm. She stumbled under his strength, but he put his arm around her waist and half-pulled, half-carried her behind the rock.

"Stay down," he said. Sariah began to cry, but Joshua shushed her. "You can't wake Hannah. I don't think they could hear her, but I'm not sure. You must be strong."

He gave her a quick hug and then stretched himself out on top of the rock to watch the scene below.

Sariah covered her face with the hem of her skirt, taking deep breaths in an effort to stop crying. The screams tore through her heart, and she put her hands over her ears, rocking back and forth and humming a tuneless sound to block out the noise.

It did no good, however. The screams and cries seemed to last forever. Then, thundering hoofs were heard again galloping from the village as the soldiers shouted triumphantly. The noise became quieter and quieter before finally fading off into the distance miles away.

Joshua slid down the rock and sat beside his wife, his head in his shaking hands. In the moonlight, Sariah could see he was pale and his dark eyes were shadowed.

Sariah clutched at his sleeve. "What did they do? What happened?" she demanded of him.

He looked up, tears glistening in his eyes.

"I think they killed the children," he said, barely able to form the words.

"But why? Why kill innocent children?" she asked, anguish in her voice.

"I don't know, I don't know." He shook his head.

His answer called forth sobs again from Sariah's chest, and he wrapped his arms around her.

"Quiet. We must be quiet for a while."

"But why would they want to kill the children?"

"I don't know, but we will stay here quietly until we are sure they are all gone, and then I will go down and see." He hesitated. "Did anyone know we were going out today?"

"No, I didn't tell anyone."

"Good. Now rest because Hannah will soon be awake and need her mother," he said.

The night turned darker, the stars blocked by clouds, and only a half moon shone down weakly on the family. Sariah had grown up playing on the hills around the village, so the usual night sounds did not frighten her. But the wails of women and angry shouts of men continued until Sariah thought she could stand them no longer.

The couple lay on the hard ground, Hannah between them. They stroked her arms as they liked to do while she slept.

"Why is she like this, Joshua?" Sariah asked. "Did we offend God?"

"Hush," Joshua said, stroking his wife's hair. "You could offend no one in your sweetness. She is our baby, and God gave her to us for a purpose. We must have faith." His hand lingered over her ear as if to muffle the sounds of the village for her. "Try to sleep."

"I can't," she said. She drew Hannah closer to her, for the first time drawing strength from her daughter, not giving it.

She finally slept as the night breeze whispered a peace to her she didn't feel. Awaking when Hannah began to stir in hunger, she found Joshua on his knees, staring at her.

"I'm going down to the village," he said. "I'll stop at Mariam's house and see what happened." He reached into the basket and got Hannah's bowl for milk and a clean cloth.

"Will you be all right?" she asked, suddenly scared again.

"Yes, it is quieter," he answered. "I'll come back before

dawn with food. You stay here with Hannah. You'll be all right."

He leaned over to kiss her on the cheek and kissed Hannah on her forehead. Blinking her eyes in drowsiness, she smiled up at her father.

"The stars will watch over you," he said. Then he was gone.

Sariah heard his footsteps down the hill for a ways, but then Hannah began to whimper, and Sariah busied herself with feeding her baby.

Dawn was just beginning to break over the hills when Joshua returned. Sariah had fallen back into a fitful sleep with Hannah in her arms but awoke as soon as she heard footsteps. Clenching Hannah to her, she held her breath until she heard him whisper, "Sariah, I'm back."

She put Hannah back on the ground gently, sat up, and held out her hands to clasp his. He knelt down on one knee across from her and held onto her hands tightly.

"Are you all right?" he asked, his eyes searching her face.

"We are," she said anxiously. "What happened? What can you tell me?"

He sat down, crossing his legs in front of him. Letting go of her hands, he put his head down and shook it.

"Oh, Sariah, it is so awful."

"What? What happened?" She stroked his hair softly, as if to coax the news from him.

He looked up with sad eyes.

"It was as I thought. The soldiers killed the babies and small children," he said slowly.

"No," she said, clasping her hands to her heart. "All of them? Why? Who did you see? Who told you?"

He put his finger on her lips.

"Too many questions at once, my sweet wife," he said. He pulled a loaf of bread from his cloak.

"Here, eat," he said, breaking her off a piece. "Mariam sent food."

"Is Mariam well?" she asked, the bread forgotten in her lap.

"As well as anyone in the village is," he said. "She was not harmed. But . . ."

He looked at her sadly again and then shook his head. "But . . ."

"Jared? Is Jared okay?" she asked, suddenly remembering her friend's sweet son.

"No. No, he is not. He is gone."

Sariah burst into sobs, and Joshua pulled her close to him and held her as she rocked back and forth in raw grief.

"All of them, Joshua, all of them?" she asked, sobbing.

"They spared some of the little girls," he said. "Mariam said they seemed to be looking for the baby boys."

"Why?"

"Mariam said the soldiers yelled above the sound of the swords that there would be no savior for Judah and that the only savior would be obedience to the Roman Empire."

Her sobs ceased and, clutching at his robe, Sariah asked, "A savior? Do they also believe there was a savior born?"

"They seem to, but . . ."

"But what? If the soldiers know of a savior, it must be so." She spoke hopefully, but those hopes were dashed as she looked up into Joshua's eyes.

"If there were a savior, God would watch over him,

although . . ." He hesitated to finish his sentence. "The soldiers said the blood ran through the streets of all Judah. How could he have survived that?"

Defeated, she now put her head in her hands and cried softly. Joshua stroked her hair and looked down at Hannah, who still slept. He was quiet for a time.

"Sariah," he said with wonder in his voice. "Sariah, why was our little baby spared? Why did God bring us to the hills last night?"

Sariah looked up from her hands and then down at her baby.

"I don't know," she answered in a whisper. "Was she really spared? Isn't her life harder since she lives? Wouldn't death be easier for one such as she?"

He pulled her into his arms again. "Where is your faith? When yours is weak, mine has no chance."

"Oh, Joshua, it's so hard," she said. "Little Jared was so happy, so sweet. To love Hannah is to know pain."

"She is happy and sweet too," he said. "We can be her arms and legs if we need to be."

"Every breath of mine is a prayer for her, but the beggars on the roads—is that the life she will have?"

"God is a god of love," he said, holding her tighter. "He gave you to me, didn't he?"

"But the others like Hannah . . ." she said.

"No more talk of that, Sariah. She is just a baby. We have no idea what the future holds for her. " He held her so tightly she could hardly breathe. "There are sorrows enough for today. We do not need tomorrow's. Now come, let's go home." He let her go.

"What if they come back?" she asked, suddenly frightened.

"I don't think that will happen. They think their evil

work is done. We must go home. Mariam will be glad to see you are safe."

Together they gathered up their meager belongings, and, with the sun hanging as a huge orange ball in the early morning sky, Joshua picked up the still-slumbering Hannah, put his arm around his wife, and guided her gently down the hill toward home.

They walked slowly, neither of them talking of their fears about what the people of the village would say when they knew that Hannah lived.

Very few paid attention to the couple who made their way down the dusty narrow street, though. Groups gathered in front of homes, sorrowing and speaking in hushed tones. From the homes the mournful keening of childless mothers could be heard. While they walked past on one side, a family came from within, the father carrying a small body wrapped in burial linens. The mother, whom Sariah had grown up with, clawed at the cloths and tried to take the baby back, as other family members restrained her, tears wetting their faces also.

Joshua handed Hannah to Sariah as they came close to the family, then wrapped his arms around her and hurried her forward. They looked down as they quickly made their way to their small home.

Sariah heard voices but couldn't understand what they said. She wanted to stop and tell them that she knew sorrow for a child too and understood somewhat of their pain, but Joshua urged her on. She looked up at him, hesitating.

"But, Joshua, these are our friends," she insisted.

"There will be time later, but we must get home safely now. Our child is alive, and they are carrying their dead one. We mustn't make their grief, or perhaps their anger, worse."

He pushed her forward.

The inside of their home was still cool from the early morning. It looked the same as it had when they left the night before, but Sariah felt no comfort in coming home. There was little protection from the harm that the soldiers could bring. Last night had proven that.

Hannah woke up as Sariah laid her down, so Sariah busied herself with changing and feeding her baby, cooing softly to her and telling her what a good girl she was. The village's grief outside seemed far away as she focused her attention on Hannah and forced herself not to think of the mothers she knew who had only empty arms that day.

Joshua paced from the door back to his wife and child, unable to settle down. His sleepless eyes were ringed by the dark circles of exhaustion.

Sariah urged him to lie down and sleep for a while, but he shook his head wordlessly, then resumed his pattern of looking out the door and returning to look down at his wife and daughter with his arms crossed and his eyebrows knit together.

With Hannah fed and clothed, Sariah picked up the water jug and went to her husband at the door, touching him on the sleeve.

"Will you watch Hannah while I bring water?" she asked.

He grabbed the jug from her.

"I'll draw the water," he said.

"But . . ." Sariah insisted, "drawing water is women's work."

"Nothing is right today," he said, kissing her on the cheek. "Stay inside."

Sariah returned to Hannah, picked her up, and began to walk around the small room, singing to her. Hannah smiled and swung her little clenched fist in her attempts to touch her mother's face.

Suddenly, Mariam burst through the door and rushed toward Sariah.

"My niece, my niece," she said, sobbing, enveloping Sariah and Hannah in a strong embrace. "You are safe. I didn't know where you were."

"We are fine," Sariah answered, trying to pull Hannah away from Mariam's suffocating squeeze. "But what about you? What of our family and friends? What happened last night? Please, tell me."

"It was awful," Mariam said, covering her face with her hands. "I cannot get the sight from my mind." She shivered in distress and couldn't finish.

"Tell me what you can," Sariah said. She pulled her aunt to the bench in front of the fireplace. "What of Joanna?"

"They are preparing Jared for burial," Mariam answered, clutching her niece's arms.

Then, haltingly, she began to relate the happenings of the night before. The two women sobbed as Mariam's memories came flooding out and horrified Sariah with their detail. Now she had a picture in her mind to accompany the screams she had heard the night before. She did not know whether to cover her ears to block the memories of the screams or her eyes to block the images of cruelty and death.

Hannah, still in Sariah's arms, looked back and forth to the mourning women until the sorrow, which she could not understand, was too much, and she also burst into sobs.

Sariah stood up and patted her back in an attempt to console her.

"Oh, baby, I am so sorry," she said. "You shouldn't have heard all that." She turned to her aunt, who was hugging her arms and rocking back and forth. "Mariam, we must be quiet for Hannah."

Mariam dried her eyes, then her tone changed to sarcasm as she looked narrowly at Sariah. "How did you know to leave the village last night? Did a star lead you away?"

Sariah stammered at the sudden shift.

"The baby . . . Hannah . . . was fretful from the heat, so we took her to the hills to find a cool breeze. She had a fever. How were we to know what was about to happen?"

Not answering her question, Mariam said, "Others wonder why some babies were saved and theirs were not."

"Joshua said the soldiers were looking for baby boys," Sariah said. "The savior that was born the night the star shone—that's whom they wanted."

"Well, that savior is dead now," Mariam said, spitting out the words. Her eyelids narrowed wickedly. "Now Joanna is without the smiles of her Jared, and Hannah lives. She would have been better off at the end of a sword."

Before Sariah could pull forth an answer from the sudden stab in her heart, Joshua stepped through the door, anger on his face.

"Enough, Mariam," he said. "You will not speak of my child that way." Taking the whimpering baby from his wife's arms, he put his strong arm around Sariah. "You are not welcome in my home if you cannot speak in love and kindness. Sariah suffers enough. Who knows the mind of God? Who knows why Hannah was spared? Do you? I think not."

Mariam shrank under his unwavering gaze, then recovered and straightened herself.

"I will go see to those who are sorrowing," she said.

Joshua motioned to the door. "You are free to go," he said. "But you are not free to return until you come with faith."

"You cannot keep me from my niece," she said, brushing past the couple.

He didn't answer until after the door had slammed, then he turned to his wife, meeting the tears in her eyes with a smile.

The evening was filled with desperate keening as the villagers buried their children. Ten in all had died—eight little boys and two baby girls.

Joshua carried Hannah and sheltered her from the gaze of others, while Sariah walked beside, torn between sorrow for the dead and gratitude that they were not burying Hannah.

When dusk began to fall and the grieving families and friends returned home, Sariah fed Hannah and put her down for the night.

"Joshua," she said, going to where he sat in front of the fire, his head in his hands. "Joshua, I must go visit Joanna. I had no chance to see her alone today."

"Please don't go out," he pleaded. "There is such sadness, and so many are angry at the children who escaped death."

"I must go," she said firmly, "and you must watch Hannah."

Looking into her determined eyes, he said a quiet yes and stroked her face. "Your resolve is only one of the many things I love about you," he said.

Sariah slipped through the door and walked the short distance down quiet streets to Joanna's house. How different the village was from the evening before at the same time when a peaceful innocence had watched over it.

When she reached Joanna's door, she knocked timidly.

Joanna's husband, Simon, opened the door. When he saw who it was, he motioned to the bed where Joanna lay sobbing, then stepped back into the shadows.

Sariah swallowed deeply, summoning up courage, and walked over to Joanna. Sitting down beside Joanna, she gathered her in her arms. Joanna saw who it was encircling her with love, and her sobs increased.

They sat for endless minutes, entwined in their grief, their tears mingling.

Simon quietly left the excruciating scene.

Finally, Sariah spoke.

"I am so sorry, my friend," she said. "I'm so sorry. Somehow God will help you through this. He is good."

"Is he?" Joanna cried against Sariah's shoulder. "Is he? If he is so good, how could he allow so many innocent lives to be taken? What did my baby do to deserve this?"

"God is not the only force in this world," Sariah said. "Surely, you cannot believe the soldiers were doing the work of God."

"I don't know," she said. She sat up and wiped her eyes. "I just know I miss my baby."

"I know it must be of no comfort, but he has gone to God," Sariah said.

They sat in silence as their tears dried, holding hands as they had done in their youth when they played the carefree games of childhood.

"Tell me something, Sariah," Joanna finally said. "How were you not in the village? How did you save Hannah?" There was no accusation in her voice, only sadness.

"I don't know why we were blessed. Hannah was feverish, and we took her to the hills where there might be a cool breeze."

"Did you know what happened?"

Sariah shivered at the memory and rubbed Joanna's hands before answering.

"We heard the screams and stayed in the hills overnight, but we didn't really know what was happening. Joshua came down to see this morning and then brought us home. He made us stay inside all day, or I would have come to see you sooner."

Joanna hugged her again. "I knew there was a reason."

She looked at Sariah as if she wanted to ask a question she didn't want to hear herself say. She finally spoke. The two young women often spoke of the whys and wherefores of life, so Joanna's question didn't surprise Sariah.

"Why was Hannah saved, Sariah?"

"I don't know," she said again, shaking her head sadly. "And what was she saved for—a life of pain and sorrow? To watch others play and not be able to join in? To be fed like a baby all the days of her life? To want to speak but have no words?"

"Oh, Sariah, I'm so sorry for your sorrow," Joanna said. "I was so happy with my Jared that I didn't always see your struggle."

"There will be plenty left to see, I believe." She looked beyond Joanna. "Remember little David who lived at the edge of the village? He looked so much like Hannah as a baby, and he never learned to walk or talk. Some think it was a blessing he died so young." She looked back at Joanna. "Mariam told me today that Hannah should have died."

Joanna shook her head in a sudden show of anger. "That woman. I don't know how you have so much patience with her. I would have barred her from my house long ago."

"I think Joshua just about did that today."

"Well, well . . . good," Joanna sputtered, bringing a smile to Sariah before they both grew silent again.

"Will I ever be happy again?" Joanna asked finally. "Will you?"

"Perhaps we will," Sariah answered. "We will have faith that we will."

They sat softly talking, one's sorrow taking up where the other's left off. They spoke of happier days they had known, storing up strength against the days ahead when life would go on and they would once again face their sadness.

4

A Gift for Hannah

Hannah turned one and then two without the days changing much. She continued to be a happy baby, although Sariah often wondered why. Still a pretty girl with big brown eyes framed by long lashes, her teeth had grown in white and straight and her dark hair, now down almost to her shoulders, fell in soft ringlets. She looked around curiously and seemed to understand everything she saw. Even though she could not speak or even babble, her big, quick smile lit up her face and earned her many smiles in return.

Thankfully, Sariah thought, although Hannah had grown longer and heavier, she remained small compared to the few other babies in the village.

She could not sit up, could not even hold her head up for more than a few seconds without it flopping one way or the other. Her arms and legs were tight and difficult to bend when Sariah had to dress her. Her hands were clenched tightly most of the time, but sometimes Sariah gently opened them up and put a soft cloth in her hand for Hannah to play with, and she would attempt to bite it or bring it up to her face to tickle her chin.

Hannah was now able to take milk from a cup, with Sariah pouring tiny sips into her mouth, being careful that she did not choke. She could even swallow thin cereal into which Sariah mixed mashed figs or tiny bits of fish or egg. It was a long, laborious process three or four times a day, but at least it gave Sariah something to do and a way to plan her days.

Often, when Hannah became unhappy and bored with her small world, Sariah carried her outside and walked up and down the street, talking to her about the sights they saw. Many people paused to touch Hannah or put their fingers inside her tight fist, bringing a smile to her face. Others would turn away as if the very sight of such an unfortunate child could somehow make their own meager lives worse.

Sariah would carry Hannah as long as she could and then reluctantly return home, her arms and often her heart aching. She tried to walk with Hannah in her arms until the baby was ready to sleep because even Hannah seemed sad when they returned and went inside. Every day, though, she had to admit painfully to herself that sometimes even her best wasn't enough to help her child.

As time passed, the evening the soldiers came became a memory too painful to bring up, and women's bellies began to bulge with new life. Sariah's didn't, however, and she often caressed her stomach as she stood in the door looking out at the others and wondering if she would be blessed with another baby. A part of her feared that she would somehow have another baby like Hannah to bring heartache to her, while the greater part longed to have a baby who would babble her name and toddle throughout the house.

She and Joanna remained close, and Joanna often came and held Hannah in the evening while Sariah and Joshua walked with their hands clasped or their arms around each other.

Mariam did not often come anymore, and Sariah had heard that she said it was too painful to see Hannah and know that God was punishing their family for some past sins she couldn't name but she knew surely must be there. Sariah thought, however, that Mariam feared Joshua and what he might do or say to tarnish her reputation as the suffering widow of the family.

On a day soon after Hannah turned two, Sariah was preparing Joshua's lunch when he burst through the door and walked quickly over to his wife.

"Close your eyes," he said, his face alight with excitement.

"Why?" she asked with a laugh. "Don't you want your lunch?"

"I have a surprise," he said, ignoring her question. He picked up Hannah off the bed and, without even hugging her and kissing her as he always did, put her in Sariah's arms. "Come outside. You'll love it."

"Do I close my eyes or walk outside? I can't do both."

He hesitated a moment.

"You're right," he said, suddenly looking serious. "All right. You stand here and close your eyes, and I'll bring it inside." He kissed Hannah, who rewarded him with a big smile. "You're going to love it, my sweet daughter."

He hurried outside as Sariah held Hannah up so she could see the surprise and then dutifully shut her eyes as he came backward through the door.

"Are they shut?" he asked.

"They are." She smiled in anticipation.

She heard something being placed with a thump on the ground before her, then Joshua took Hannah from her.

"Open your eyes," he said proudly.

She did, and there before her was a tiny wagon with four wheels and a long handle. The sides were built up on one end, and soft blankets were draped over the end.

"I made Hannah a wagon," he said proudly. "Now you can take her out more easily." Shifting Hannah to one arm, he picked up one of the handles and moved the wagon back and forth a few inches, demonstrating how easy it was to use. "Don't you think she will love it? You can go for walks every day and go to the market." He waited expectantly and then added, "I hope you like it."

Sariah was speechless, her hands over her open mouth. Tears came to her eyes.

"Oh, Joshua, it is wonderful," she said.

"So you do like it?"

"I love it." Jumping into his free arm, she hugged him and Hannah tightly. "It will be so good for her." She pulled away and, putting her hands back up to her mouth, shook her head at the surprise.

Joshua leaned Hannah over so she could see her new wagon. "You can go outside now, Hannah, on long walks with us."

He tickled her gently and she laughed. Sariah knelt down and ran her hands over the polished wood. Joshua had obviously spent many hours on the finish, making sure not even one tiny splinter could hurt Hannah. She rocked back on her heels.

"It is beautiful," she said.

"I got the wood from a passing merchant," he said. "He gave me a fair price when he heard what I was going to do with it. He said it was really nice wood."

"It's perfect," she said. "I can go to the market again and go visit Joanna and . . . do anything."

Standing up, she hugged her husband again and kissed him solidly on the mouth. "I love you, Joshua."

"And I you," he said. "Here, let's put her in it." Bending down, he nestled the baby into the blankets. She looked around at the sides and reached out with her fists to touch the softness, then she smiled up at her parents.

"Look, Hannah, look what it can do," Joshua said. He picked up the handle and ever so gently began to pull.

At first, it startled her and she looked up with fear in her eyes but met only the reassuring smiles of her parents.

"It's fine, Hannah," Sariah said, reaching down and patting her. "Your father made it for you. You will love it."

Joshua pulled her around the room, laughing and making faces at her until she squealed in delight.

"Listen to her," he said. "She does love it."

Sariah clapped her hands and laughed. She felt like new light had just come into her life. Suddenly, the walls of the house that at times seemed like a prison to her glowed with light and possibilities.

Then, watching the joy of her child and husband, she returned to finish preparing their meal.

"Come, eat, Joshua," she said, sitting down at the table. "Bring her to me."

"Here we come," he said. He pulled the wagon next to Sariah, and, holding her behind her head with one strong hand, he kissed the top of her soft hair.

She reached up and clasped his hand. "Your surprise has given me great joy," she said, "as you always give me. Thank you."

He sat down and said, "After the evening meal, we will go throughout the village to visit."

He looked down at Hannah, who still sat smiling, her head tipped to one side, drool dripping from her mouth.

"We will walk tonight under the stars, my sweet daughter,"

he said, "under the stars that gave you life."

They did walk under the starlight that evening, down the streets of the village, pulling the wagon with a smiling Hannah burrowed in the blankets. Joshua was careful to avoid the rocks and to walk slowly so as not to frighten her. Sariah walked beside him, both of them turning every few seconds to make sure she was all right.

The tiny marketplace was quiet, but neighbors on the narrow street stood in their doors and happily watched the small procession. Sariah felt a new sense of freedom out in the fresh air of the sunset.

She even sang softly under her breath, until they reached the outskirts of the village where the way became rockier.

"What if it tips over, Joshua?" Sariah worried.

"It won't. I made it very sturdy as long as you do not go too fast."

"All right," she said, then was quiet for a few minutes.

"What will we do when she outgrows it?" she asked as they left the streets of the town and headed down the dusty road.

"Then I will make her a larger one."

"And when she outgrows that?"

"A still larger one," he said, his voice rising slightly.

"And when she outgrows that?"

He slowed his pace and grabbed her hand, looking down on her, a frown furrowing his brow.

"What are you asking, pretty one?"

"What will we do when we are old, and she is big?" Her voice began to quiver. "What is her future? I cannot stand to think of her begging by the wayside, dirty and hungry."

"Then don't think of it because it will not happen," he said. "God has already saved her twice. Will he not save her again? Where is your faith?" He looked off into the distance, his eyes cloudy.

"Don't be mad at me," she pleaded. "Most of the time, my faith is here, but sometimes I must search to find it. I just want to know."

"It wouldn't be faith if it were always there and you always knew," he said. "God gives people like us faith. To the prophets he gives knowledge."

Quiet again for a moment, Sariah looked up at him hopefully as they slowly turned back to the village, the wagon wheels crunching on the road behind them.

"Is there any news of the savior?" she asked. "Was he killed that night, or did he also escape as our Hannah did?"

"The shepherds I have seen know nothing of what happened to the baby born that night in Bethlehem," he said, "but if the baby born was indeed the savior, I am sure God saved him as he did Hannah."

"And he will save us. He can make Hannah well."

"See, there is your faith. It was close by."

"It is easy with you around," she said, pure love on her face as she looked up at him.

"Then I will always be here." He stopped and, smiling down at Hannah, put his arms around his wife, buried his head in her hair, and whispered, "As long as I have breath in my body, I will take care of you and Hannah."

She hugged him back, feeling his strength that readily called forth her faith. For one moment, she could believe all would be well.

5

An Accidental Encounter

That feeling was short-lived, however. By the next week, Sariah had learned how to negotiate the wagon herself and spent her mornings and late afternoons pulling it up and down the streets, taking Hannah to visit the neighbors. Most of the people were overjoyed to see Sariah and Hannah out in the sunlight with smiles on their faces. A few saw them making their way down the street and quickly went into their homes, shutting the doors behind them. Sariah stayed away from those homes. She also made sure not to go down the street where Mariam lived.

One afternoon, though, she was not able to avoid her aunt. She had stopped at Joanna's home and invited her to join them. Heavy with child, Joanna at first had said she was too tired, but with Sariah's begging and Hannah's obvious joy at being out on a walk, Joanna finally gave in and agreed to walk with them, albeit slowly.

Down the dirt street they walked, laughing at Joanna's cumbersome gait, with small houses crowding together on either side. The warmth of the afternoon had driven most people in, but Sariah thought the fresh air felt wonderful. The smells of early supper preparation wafted through the dusty air.

Before Sariah realized it, they had reached the end where to turn right would take them to Mariam's house. Sariah slowed to cross over to the other side of the street, but was not fast enough. Mariam came around the corner, almost bumping into them.

Sariah quickly stopped the wagon, reaching out to steady Joanna, who had moved aside to avoid being hit. Mariam recovered and looked at the group, her nose up in the air.

"Why, good afternoon, Mariam," Sariah said with as much friendliness as she could muster, even though her heart began to beat faster at the sight of her aunt. She stepped in between Mariam and the wagon, unconsciously shielding Hannah from her.

"What are you doing here?" Mariam asked as if she owned the street.

"We're out for a walk," Sariah answered, standing solid, even though Mariam attempted to look behind her.

"Where is that . . . that child of yours?" Mariam asked. She stepped to the side where she could see the wagon and Hannah lying still and looking all around her.

Sariah and Joanna glanced at each other warily.

"What is that?" Mariam demanded in disgust, gesturing to the wagon.

Sariah stretched herself up as tall as she could get, and Joanna grabbed her hand in support.

"It's a wagon that Joshua made so that Hannah could come

outside," Sariah explained quietly.

Mariam's eyes narrowed and glittered with a dark meanness. Her mouth was a lipless slit.

"How dare you bring her out and flaunt her in front of my friends," she said. "Have you no shame at all?"

With her heart beating so loudly she thought Mariam must be able to hear it, Sariah bravely stuck her chin out.

"I have done nothing to be ashamed of, Mariam," she said. "Hannah is my daughter, and I love her."

"Love has nothing to do with it," Mariam said indignantly. She was breathing heavily and took a step toward Sariah, who stepped back, still keeping herself between Mariam and the wagon.

But Mariam was the larger woman, and when she took her arm and pushed her aside, Sariah stumbled and fell into Joanna, who instinctively protected her bulging belly with one arm and reached out for the support of the nearest wall with the other. Sariah fell to her knees and cried out in pain as she caught herself with her hands, twisting her wrist.

As Mariam stepped closer and bent over the wagon, though, Sariah ignored the pain, crawled the short distance to the wagon, and pulled herself up. Mariam was spitting words into Hannah's face.

"I should have let you die that night," she growled at Hannah.

Hannah, who had never been spoken to harshly in her life, jerked her head around and looked up with big eyes that were first full of question and then fear.

"Leave her alone," Sariah yelled, grabbing Mariam's arm.

But Mariam easily pulled it away and clasped Hannah's arm that was flailing in the air in defense.

"What was your parents' sin for you to be born so afflicted?"

she continued, holding Hannah's arm down. "Maybe a star will appear again and mercifully let you die."

As Hannah began to whimper, Sariah lunged toward Mariam, pushing her away from Hannah. Surprised, Mariam let go of Hannah's arm.

"Get away from her," she yelled at Mariam.

The force of her protectiveness won out over the large woman, and Mariam stepped back, pure hatred on her face.

"Why are you doing this?" Sariah demanded. "We haven't done anything to you."

"You have brought disgrace upon our family," she growled.

Torn between comforting Hannah, who was now screaming, or answering her aunt's accusations, Sariah chose the former. She knelt down beside Hannah and spoke soothingly to her, rubbing her arm where the marks of Mariam's hands were beginning to bruise.

Then, looking up at Mariam, she took a calming breath and said, "I find no disgrace in loving my child. I'm sorry you cannot see that."

Standing up and reaching for the handles of the wagon again, she winced at the pain in her wrist.

She glanced over at a pale Joanna and said, "Come, Joanna, let's go home."

Mariam glared at them but said nothing more as they turned the wagon around and slowly headed back down the street.

Later that evening, Sariah related the events of the afternoon to Joshua as she sat across from him and rested her bandaged wrist on the table. Joshua said very little, but Sariah knew by his clenched jaw that he would not let Mariam get away with what she had said.

He stood up as she finished her tale and looked down at her.

"Go rest," he said. "I am going to go talk to Mariam."

She put her uninjured hand on his arm.

"Don't cause even more trouble," she said.

"She will not say such things about our daughter," he said firmly. "We did nothing wrong to bring her into the world as she is. Somehow it is God's will, and we must trust in that. Even if Mariam cannot see that, she will not hurt you or Hannah."

He bent down to kiss her, then quietly walked out of the house. She realized that it would do no good to call him back, and a part of her was glad to know that.

Sariah was lying awake in the dark when Joshua came back and sat down beside her.

"She won't bother you again," he said.

"Is she all right?" Sariah asked. "You didn't hurt her, did you?"

"Of course not." He laughed softly. "Even if I wanted to. She could hear the smile in his voice as he continued, "Let's just say that I have never heard Mariam speechless before."

6

Questions with No Answers

Over the next five years, Sariah and Joanna became as close as if they were sisters. Joanna gave birth to two little girls, while Sariah's arms remained empty. She didn't resent Joanna for her blessings, however, knowing that Joanna would always hold pain close in her heart for the brutal loss of her baby Jared.

The two would walk through the village to the market and down to the well, pulling Hannah with Joanna carrying her baby Deborah and little Rachel toddling behind. Often, when they tired of picking Rachel up and drying her tears as she tripped, they sat her in the end of the wagon at Hannah's feet.

Hannah would answer with screams of joy as she accepted her small responsibility of watching over the baby. Her legs, thin and crossed, would quiver with excitement, and her arms draw up tightly against her bony chest. She had learned to make a sound that Sariah recognized as "Muh, Muh," and Sariah knew she was being called to soothe her daughter or to guess which of her simple needs she should attend to. She called her father "Puh, Puh" in a sound that brought a smile to his lips.

As much time as Sariah spent feeding her, Hannah still remained thin. Sariah easily lifted her and never complained of her back aching, although some nights she found it hard to find a comfortable position to sleep.

Hannah remained pretty with long brown curls that hung down over the back of her wagon and eyes that seemed to look through people with a purpose they could never understand. When Sariah looked into the eyes of her daughter, she felt like the answers to all the questions that drove Sariah to her knees in desperate prayer were there, but somewhere between Hannah's eyes and her straining mouth, the message was lost.

Hannah's understanding remained simple, but her curiosity and interest in the life of the village was strong. Sariah knew by the light in her eyes that she recognized those people who were good to her. She only hoped she did not hear or understand those who weren't.

Often, as they walked, people would remark on Hannah's beauty, then add with a "tsk" that it really was sad that her life was what it was since she was so pretty.

"Would they deny my daughter of all of God's blessings?" Sariah asked Joanna as they walked one spring afternoon. Winding through the village, they had chanced upon Aunt Mariam and one of her friends, who had remarked on the futility of Hannah's looks when her life had no hope of being anything more than what it was now.

Mariam had smirked as if she had thought it but not said it. Sariah was sure she had seen just a glimpse of sorrow in Mariam's eyes, however, as she looked upon her niece and knew her friend's remark had caused her pain.

"We are just fine," Sariah had retorted and pulled the wagon away with as much indignity as she could muster.

"I really wanted to scratch her eyes out," Sariah said to Joanna when they were out of earshot.

They made their way along the path to the well. Rachel had fallen asleep in the wagon, and Hannah watched carefully, having been given the charge to call for her mother if Rachel woke. Baby Deborah watched the wagon over her mother's shoulder.

"You? You are much too sweet for that," Joanna answered with a laugh.

"Me?" Sariah replied. "I do not think of myself as sweet."

"That husband of yours always calls you his 'sweet Sariah,'" Joanna replied.

"Oh, that's just Joshua," Sariah said with a wave of her hand. His attentions were so consistently loving that, though she never demanded them, they were part of the fabric of her marriage.

Joanna stopped and faced Sariah on the path, putting her hand on her friend's arm.

"Can't you see yourself as others see you?"

Sariah brought the wagon to a stop behind them and looked at her, puzzled.

"How is that?" she asked. "An object of pity? Or crazy—a believer in a miracle of a bright star? Or is it the faithless Sariah who believes but cannot work a miracle in the life of her own daughter?"

Her words rushed out of her as if her heart would empty in a flood of emotions that would drain into the dry dirt of the desert, sinking to cause her heartache no more.

"No, Sariah," Joanna said slowly. "They see a faithful, strong, gentle, quiet mother who tends to her daughter like an angel would. They see patience."

"Patience in suffering," Sariah said in a rare moment of self-pity.

"I'm not sure many see the suffering because you are so good at hiding it."

"Perhaps," Sariah said. "Doesn't that make me a hypocrite then?" She smiled softly.

"No, you are my dear friend, Sariah," Joanna said. She handed the baby over to Sariah. "Here, you hold her for a while, and I will pull the wagon. Perhaps I can't remove the load from your soul, but I can help shoulder the burden of pulling Hannah."

Sariah smelled the sweetness of the baby and let her wrap her tiny fingers around her thumb.

"Why am I denied another baby, Joanna?" she asked thoughtfully. "Couldn't God bless me with the happiness of seeing a child of mine crawl and talk and walk to me?"

Joanna carefully held the wagon back as the road began to slope down gently.

"You are good at asking questions I can't answer," she said.

"I beg God nightly that he will send me another baby. He answered the prayers of my namesake Sarah and blessed her with a baby."

"Would you like to become a mother again at ninety?" Joanna chided gently.

Sariah considered that for a moment, then laughed. "Ask me when I am eighty-nine," she said.

The mood lightening, Joanna said, "By then, you will be pulling me in the wagon."

"I would do that."

"Yes, you would, Sariah," Joanna said, slowing down to look over fondly at her friend, "and that is what I love about you."

Suddenly a cry was heard from the wagon, followed by a strained, "Muh, Muh."

The women turned to see Rachel rubbing her eyes sleepily. Hannah was straining with every muscle in her body to move her arms and legs with clumsy jerks to tell her mother that her charge had awoken.

As Joanna reached for Rachel, Sariah looked with pride at Hannah.

"What a helper you are, Hannah!" she exclaimed. "I knew you would call us when the baby woke up."

Hannah beamed as best she could, turning her head from side to side in excitement.

"Thank you so much, Hannah," Joanna said. "She might have fallen out of the wagon if not for you."

To Hannah's delight, Sariah put baby Deborah in the wagon and bent down to first kiss Hannah, then wipe her wet chin. Pulling her back up in the wagon, she rearranged the blankets so no knot of discomfort would touch her daughter.

As the sun began to dip in the western sky, the little group slowly wended its way to the well.

7

Trying to Remember

Days passed with numbing sameness in the village. Nights were dark when the moon was not full, and people slept to the lullaby of the bleating of the nearby sheep. When dawn began to break, a rooster at the edge of the village would call everyone to awake, and the life that they had lived the day before began again.

Sariah awoke every morning at the crowing and prepared herself for the day before Joshua and Hannah stirred. By the time they opened their eyes, Sariah had set Joshua's meal out and cooked a thin cereal that she could drip into Hannah's mouth. Sometimes, Sariah and Joshua had a few minutes to themselves before they heard Hannah, but usually as soon as she heard the voice of her father, she would call out, and they would rush to her side.

Feeding Hannah was a long task that left about as much cereal on her as in her stomach, so when Joshua left for the blacksmith shop, Sariah would take the water that had been heating beside the fire and gently bathe her daughter. She knelt beside her every morning and sang soft songs to her as she tugged on her tight arms and legs to wash her. She washed her face and told her of the light that came into her eyes the night the star had shone upon her and God had given them their precious daughter.

No matter how many times Sariah told her that story, Hannah would stare at her mother, enraptured, until the end of the story when the newborn Hannah opened her eyes and smiled up at her mother.

"We must believe, Hannah, that you are a gift from God," Sariah said. "Do you believe, Hannah?"

At that, Hannah would nod her head as best she could.

"I know you believe," Sariah said. "And I know the angels speak to you and tell you of God's love for you, don't they, Hannah?"

She would nod again, and Sariah, whose faith might have faltered since the morning before, believed once again.

When Hannah was eleven, Sariah began to sew for the villagers, hoping not only to save a few coins for the needs of their small family but to have an opportunity to visit with the women as they came to collect the clothes she had carefully fashioned. She was known for her tiny, neat stitches and often purchased ribbons from traveling merchants, adding those around the hem or sleeves to the delight of her customers.

As she sewed beneath the light of the window, she laid Hannah beside her, propped up so that she might watch her mother sew. Sariah had stitched together a crude doll for Hannah, which she kept tightly clenched throughout the day in her arm. When Sariah would ask her if she loved her baby, Hannah smiled and pulled the baby close, straining to reach her head down to her.

Often, Sariah would pick the softest ribbons and open Hannah's hands to hold one. With difficulty, Hannah could raise her hand up to touch the ribbon to her face. The process took several minutes and left her exhausted with the effort but proud that she had accomplished the small task.

Hour followed hour, which turned into days that followed days. Often, Sariah's throat would be hoarse after a day of talking and singing to her daughter. Her back began to ache from her relentless work bent over her needle and from caring for Hannah, who still remained thin and smaller than others her age, but grew longer with arms and legs that would not cooperate when she was picked up.

The best days were those when the women of the village— and those of other villages as word of Sariah's talent spread— came to pick up their clothing. Some of them, unsure of what to do around Hannah, would take their clothing as quickly as possible, press a few coins into Sariah's palm, and hurry out, with eyes averted from the child who squirmed and struggled unsuccessfully to speak at the joy of having someone new to look at in their small home.

Others were kinder and took time to bend over Hannah's place of honor on her pallet and speak to her, pretending they could understand the grunts and moans Hannah could make.

"Did you help your mother make this, Hannah?" the women said. "It is so pretty. I think you are a good helper."

Hannah would squeal loudly and attempt to nod her head, until her doll would slip from her arms and her clothes were mussed from her moving.

Sariah loved those women and made sure the stitches on their garments were even straighter and smaller. She would gladly have paid them to let her do their work in exchange for the small amount of attention paid to her child.

On days when the sun shone down warmly on the village and the birds sang, Sariah would put Hannah in her wagon outside the front door that was shaded with a canopy Joshua had fashioned so Hannah could be outside without the sun burning her delicate skin. Sariah would pull a cushion to the door and sit there, her sewing baskets around her, and stitch in the fresh air. Those days were good, for she almost felt a part of the community and, when Hannah was quiet or drowsed in the sunshine, she could imagine her life was normal like those of the women who worked outside as their children laughed and ran under their feet.

Sariah grew to accept her aunt's refusal to be a part of their lives and no longer felt hurt from it. Her capacity for heart-ache was full as she watched other girls Hannah's age grow into beautiful young girls and giggle together as pairs of them walked down the street, smiling at the young men whose atten-tions they began to notice. She tried to imagine Hannah as one of them, but gave up when the pain was too much to bear. She felt guilty when she doubted the wisdom and goodness of God and the lot of Hannah's life he had meted out. At these times, she struggled to capture her faith again.

Watching the stars at night when the sky was deep and clear, she tried to recall the memory of the night that the star brought her child to life. "Remember, God," she would whis-per, her hands clutched in prayer to her chest. "Remember, and show me what the miracle was meant to be." However hard she listened and looked, though, no star shone brighter than another and no voice answered her prayer. She waited, she watched, she asked, but it was left to her memory and her heart to feel the hope of that special night so long ago.

8

A New Heartache

One morning Sariah sewed outside as Joanna sat beside her, watching her children build a village with the rocks in the road. To Hannah's delight, Joanna rocked her wagon gently and brushed her face with a piece of soft cloth.

The women spoke of the matters of the village—who would be marrying in the next few months and of the babies that had been born and the old people they had known since their youth who were ailing.

It was a morning like many mornings before and, though Sariah tried not to think about them, would be like many mornings ahead.

"Who do you think will be the fortunate one to have one of your daughters as a wife?" Sariah asked Joanna, making a face at Hannah to hear her laugh.

"There is no one good enough for my daughters. Their father said he will keep them home forever to live with us until worthy men come and ask for their hands."

"Doesn't he get tired of four girls in the house telling him what to do?"

"He only gets tired of my telling him what to do. The girls can do no wrong."

"He's a good man. You did well in marrying him."

"As you did with Joshua." Joanna looked kindly upon her friend. "He still adores you, even though . . ." She suddenly leaned forward and looked closely at Sariah's scalp. "Is that a gray hair I see on your head?"

Sariah dropped her sewing and clutched her head with both hands. "No, it can't be. Pull it out."

Joanna laughed at her reaction. "My dear friend, you have already turned thirty, and I have just a few weeks to go. I imagine we will both see a lot of gray hairs soon."

Sariah tipped her head toward Joanna.

"How many do you see?" she asked. "Is it many?"

Suddenly, an awful noise interrupted their conversation. The two women turned from their playfulness to see Hannah's head turned to one side and straining at the neck. Her arms were flailing in the air, and, as they watched, her face turned deathly white.

They both stood up and leaned over her, their hearts clutched with fear, looking for any reason she would act in such a way.

"Hannah, Hannah," Sariah said, shaking her. "What's wrong?"

Hannah continued to struggle, then began to grit her teeth. Her whole body shook violently, as if she contended against some unseen enemy.

Time slowed. Sariah could get Hannah to neither look at nor respond to her. She knelt down beside the wagon and grabbed her up as best she could, although Hannah's stiff, thrashing arms made it difficult to embrace her. Sariah began to sob. "Hannah, Hannah," she screamed. But nothing brought

Hannah's attention back. She was lost somewhere Sariah could not reach.

"Go get Joshua," Joanna said to Deborah. "Quickly. Run."

The little girl started to run down the street, sobs breaking from her chest.

Joanna leaned over Sariah with her arm around her as Hannah shook in Sariah's arms.

"God, help me," Sariah prayed over and over, willing whatever demon possessed Hannah to let go of her.

A small group began to gather from the nearby houses, filled with women covering their mouths with their hands and children hiding in their mothers' skirts. Sariah was not aware of them, however.

Then, as suddenly as she'd begun, Hannah stopped shaking and lay limp in Sariah's arms, pale, blood mingling with drool on her white cheeks.

"Hannah," Sariah called. She looked at Joanna desperately. "Is she breathing?" She laid her back down and, grabbing her face, shook her gently. "Hannah!" she called louder. Still her child did not respond.

"She is breathing," Joanna said, her hand on Hannah's chest.

Sariah rocked back and forth on her knees, crying.

Joshua suddenly pushed through the small crowd and knelt down beside Sariah.

"What's wrong?" he asked, his own face pale, his chest struggling for breath after running through the village. He looked back and forth at his wife—who sobbed in distress—and his daughter, her head rolled back and her eyelids barely open.

Sariah could not speak, so Joanna put her hand on his arm.

"We were sitting here and Hannah began to shake and struggle. It seemed to last forever."

He bent down to touch Hannah.

"Let's take her inside," he said. He scooped his daughter into his arms and stood. Sariah still knelt on the ground.

"Joanna, bring Sariah," he directed.

Joanna pulled Sariah up from the ground, and they followed Joshua into the house. He gently laid Hannah on her bed. Color had returned somewhat to her face, but she looked up at her father with no recognition in her eyes.

"Get a wet cloth for her," Joshua told Sariah, who stood lost before him. He smiled down at her and touched her on the shoulder. "It will be all right. Bring her a cloth."

His calmness urged her back from the edge of fear. She hurried to the water jug and returned with a cool, damp rag. Then she joined Joshua where he knelt holding Hannah's hand and began to bathe her face and arms gently.

Her lip began to swell where her teeth had gnashed her mouth.

Slowly, she returned from beyond the vacant stare in her eyes and, sighing deeply, focused her eyes on her mother and managed a weak smile.

"Are you all right, Hannah?" Sariah said. "Do you hurt?"

Hannah barely shook her head in answer and lay quietly as color returned to her face and her limbs began to relax. Seemingly exhausted, she drifted off to sleep under the watchful eyes of her parents.

"How is she?" Joanna asked from behind Sariah where she had been watching the whole time. Her little girls were lined up on the bench, eyes wide and wondering.

"Her color is good, and she's sleeping," Joshua said, watching her closely.

"What happened, Joshua?" Sariah asked. "There was no cause. She was lying there happily."

"I don't know," he said, but with a reluctance in his voice that worried Sariah.

"What are you not telling me?" she demanded in a whisper. She grabbed his arm and squeezed it as if she could force an answer from him.

"I don't know," he said, shrugging his shoulders. "It may be nothing." He gently removed her hand from his arm and held it.

"What? Tell me," she demanded.

The words came slowly. "There was a man who came to the shop from the city one day to have a yoke made. When he heard of Hannah, he told me of a man he knew who had been lame from birth and would fall to the ground in fits and shake until he was pale and exhausted."

Sariah's fear returned at the thought of this happening to her child again. "What happened to him?"

"He is still alive, I think," he said, not wanting to discourage her. "I haven't seen the man who told me for a while."

Dread filled her eyes. "So this will happen again?"

He shrugged his shoulders. "That I don't know."

He put his arm around her, and she buried her head in his shoulder. When she spoke, he could hardly hear her. "How much more can she bear?"

"I don't know, my beautiful Sariah. I don't know." Joshua's tears wet the top of Sariah's head. "But look—she is sleeping quietly now."

Slipping from his grasp, Sariah sank to the bed beside her daughter and curled up next to her, her eyes closed and tears seeping from between her eyelids.

Joshua looked over to Joanna in a mute plea for help, but

Joanna could only cry silently and look back at him with no answers.

She left her daughters and, touching Joshua's arm as she walked by, knelt down beside Sariah and put her hand on her shoulder.

"Sariah, I have to take the children home," she said. "Send Joshua if you need me. You know I am only a cry or a prayer away."

Sariah turned and smiled in acknowledgement but said nothing.

Joanna left, nudging her children out the door before her.

Joshua stood over his wife and child, helpless to ease Sariah's pain, which was mirrored in his own heart as he watched Hannah peacefully slumber.

Hannah slept throughout most of the day as her parents remained watchful by her side. She was calm and smiling when she awoke, but willingly slept again as darkness crept up on the village.

Exhausted, Joshua lay down early and fell deeply into sleep before Sariah gave up her own exhausting vigil beside Hannah.

He awoke later in the dark as suddenly as he had fallen asleep and knew by the depth of the darkness that the night was still young. Sariah wasn't beside him, and, rubbing his eyes in fatigue, he didn't see her beside Hannah either.

Struggling up from the bed, he first knelt down by Hannah's pallet and saw that her eyes were still closed. A lamp burned weakly by the hearth, so he raised the wick until the light shone throughout the house and revealed that his wife was nowhere to be seen.

He stepped outside the door and looked up and down the quiet street until he thought he heard crying. Listening in every direction, he determined the pitiful sounds came from their roof and quietly ascended the stairs at the side of the house. He reached the top and paused, seeing Sariah kneeling in the middle of the roof, so intent on her prayers that she didn't even hear him close by.

She knelt with arms folded and head down, crying as she pleaded with God to look down upon her and hear her prayers for her daughter.

"Please, dear God," she said between sobs. "Hear me, thy humble handmaiden. Bless my daughter this night as thou blessed her with life the night that thy star shone down upon her. Spare her from any more pain and unhappiness than is already her lot in life. Bless me with strength to care for her and love her."

Joshua looked on her as long as his heart could stand the sight, and then, with his own heart aching and pleading with God not only for his daughter but for the wife he loved more than he loved himself, he dropped to one knee and bowed his head also.

His prayers mingled with Sariah's until finally, her prayers spent, she lay on the hard floor and cried weakly.

He crept over to her and gathered her up in his arms. She melted into him, and they wept together.

"I try, Joshua. I try," she whispered.

"And God knows," he answered, stroking her hair.

"Does he? Does he even know we are here? What does he require of me?"

Silent for a moment, he finally replied, "He knew where to send his star, didn't he?"

She seemed to consider that, then sighed. "It has been a long time since that star."

For that he had no answer, and so they stayed under the stars that did not send down any healing light that night until concern for Hannah once more beckoned them down to her side. There, arms wrapped around each other, they looked down at her and drew strength from their love for her.

9

Joshua's Trip

Hannah's twelfth year was a difficult one, filled with dread for those times when she would lose control of her arms and legs and be thrown violently about in some world her parents did not know. When she rested after a spell, there was relief and gratitude for a while until the next time of fear was upon them.

Exhaustion battled with discouragement within Sariah and, before her time, her hair turned grayer and wrinkles of worry began to line her brow. Joshua still held her tenderly and whispered to her of her beauty.

One sunny day before Passover, Joshua came home with excitement in his eyes. He found Sariah on her knees, bathing Hannah's forehead as she lay pale and weak on her bed.

"Again?" he asked his wife, knowing from the unshed tears in her eyes how her afternoon had been spent. He knelt down beside her and, stealing the cloth from Sariah, took over the task.

They stayed there quietly until, a few minutes later, Joshua said, "Look, the color is back in her cheeks."

A few minutes later, after Hannah closed her eyes, Joshua turned to his wife, unable to mask his excitement any longer.

"I have to tell you of a decision I have made," he said.

She smiled tiredly up at him. "Will I like it?"

"I think so," he said. "Come, sit with me. Hannah is sleeping now."

He lifted Sariah up and led her to the table where they sat down before it on cushions, a look of curiosity on her face.

"I am going to Jerusalem for the Passover, and I will make sacrifices and offer prayers for Hannah."

She gasped and put her hand to her mouth. They had not gone to Jerusalem since they had had Hannah. Sariah would not leave her, and Joshua would not leave Sariah while he made the journey that took several hours by foot.

"What do you think?" He looked at her expectantly, seeking approval.

Tears rose in her eyes.

"Don't cry," he said, grabbing her hand. "I . . . I guess I don't have to go."

"No," she said quickly. "Don't mistake my tears for unhappiness. I think what you are doing is good. In fact, I'll make you new clothes to go because I know God will hear your prayers at the temple."

"He hears our prayers now. You know that." He squeezed her hand.

"I do," she reassured him. "But . . ." She jumped up. "I'll begin now. You'll look so splendid that the crowds will part and let you through first to the temple."

She walked over and picked up a small jug beside the hearth. Smiling mysteriously at him, she rattled it, and he heard the clinking of coins.

He laughed. "Why, I think my wife has been saving up

money without my knowing it."

"I have," she said excitedly. She began to shake the coins onto the table, and they made a nice pile when she had finished.

"What have you been saving for?" He grabbed her around the waist with his hands and pulled her down to his lap.

"I don't know," she admitted. "I just had a feeling that I should, and so I've put a few coins away each time I sell some clothing to a rich woman. Now I know why I have been saving. I'll make you clothes so that you will be the most handsome man in Jerusalem, and you can buy the most perfect doves, or even a sheep, for a sacrifice."

Suddenly she furrowed her brow and stared at him through narrowed eyes.

"What's wrong?" he asked.

"Perhaps I don't want you to be the most handsome man in Jerusalem since I will not be there," she said, reaching up to touch his face.

"Don't worry. You have my heart always and forever." He kissed her affectionately on the lips, then sat back and stared at her. "Are you sure you will be all right without me? I will be gone about four days. Can Joanna stay with you?"

She slapped him gently on the chest. "Of course I'll be all right. Joanna has her own family, but I can always go to her if I need her."

"I'll ask her to watch over you and Hannah." He hugged Sariah tightly.

"We'll be fine, Joshua. Don't worry." She stood and scooped up some of the coins. "It's time for Ishmael to come again, and I'll buy cloth then." She put the rest of the coins back in the jug. "You may have the rest for the temple."

Suddenly growing serious, he looked at her and asked, "What do you hope will happen, Sariah? I don't want you to be even more burdened with disappointment after my trip."

"I don't know," she answered, refusing to let go of her joy. "I don't know. But even if Hannah does not get well through your prayers and sacrifices, you need to go. Something good will happen. I feel it."

He still looked doubtful, and she saw it.

Speaking deliberately, she said, "Now it is my turn to tell you to have faith. It will be good. Whatever happens, going to the temple of God will be good for us."

"You're right," he said. He whispered again as he watched her return the jug to its place and turn once again to Hannah. "You are right. Something good will happen."

The two weeks before Joshua left for the temple were busier than usual for Sariah. A thread of excitement ran through her mundane days as she prepared for her husband to go to Jerusalem.

"Your daddy is going to see the temple of God," she explained to Hannah as she fed her a week before Joshua was to leave. "When he's there, he'll offer sacrifices and say prayers that God will bless our family."

Hannah laughed, spraying cereal all over Sariah, and shook her tight arms in the air in glee—the way she always did when her mother spoke to her with happiness in her voice.

Sariah wiped the cereal off of her and laughed herself. "You are excited, aren't you? Maybe one day, we can go to the temple with your father also." Her eyes got big, and she bent down to whisper in Hannah's ear. "We'll tell your father to go before us and find a place so that we may go there also when you are better. It will be a glorious journey."

In the joy of the moment, Sariah grabbed her daughter up around her shoulders and rocked back and forth over the bed, both of them laughing.

Then Sariah thought perhaps Hannah would choke from her laughing, or, worse, go into a fit, so she laid her gently back down and said with mock sternness, "Now, Hannah, you must eat and keep up your strength so that you may make that journey."

Hannah nodded her head as best she could in obedience and with difficulty said, "Puh, puh."

"You're right, my sweet—your handsome father is going to the temple." Patting Hannah to calm her down so she could eat, Sariah began to sing to her. She was rewarded with a big smile and an open mouth for the bowl of cereal.

Throughout the days that followed, Sariah kept up a constant conversation with Hannah as she sewed Joshua new clothes from fine muslin she had purchased when the merchant Ishmael, wearing jewels on every finger and a silk turban on his head, had come by their small house soon after Joshua had announced his plans. When she had told him what she wanted, he had looked at Hannah and winked.

"So the father of this pretty girl is going to Jerusalem," he said with a belly laugh that always startled Hannah. "We must have him looking like a king." From his pack, he pulled out cloth that Sariah knew she could not afford, but he squeezed his eyes together and, pretending to figure in his mind, named a price she knew was far too little.

She contemplated his offer, feeling like she was cheating a good man, then looked over to where he had placed a pretty, tiny bracelet on Hannah's wrist with obvious delight. Wanting the fabric badly, she decided the decision to accept his offer would bring him happiness, and quickly, before she changed her mind, said, "Yes, I will take it."

"Delightful," he said. "And now this pretty young lady here has fallen in love with this bracelet, and it just so happens that the special this day is a bracelet with every bolt of cloth purchased."

"But . . ." Sariah began to protest at his obvious generosity.

He stopped her with a fat finger to his lips. "Bolts of cloth I have many, but how often do I see a smile like that?" He nodded his head toward Hannah, who lay in her wagon with her arm up in the air so she could watch, enraptured, as the trinket sparkled in the sunlight.

"Do not deny an old man an occasional pleasure," he said.

Sariah smiled, the material clasped to her chest. "You are a good man."

"And you," he said, turning to leave, "are a good mother."

She had no answer to that, so, laying down her purchase, she went over to Hannah and waved her arm in farewell to the kind trader.

It took Sariah days and days to stitch together Joshua's tunic and cloak. She spent hours in front of the house with Hannah beside her in the wagon, using the sunlight to sew tiny stitches—the tiniest and straightest she had ever done. To her, the labor was one of sacrifice and love, almost as if it were her sacrifice at the temple.

Hannah lay in her wagon, dozing or watching her mother. Sariah talked and sang to her until her throat became raw. Joanna came often and watched the progress of the sewing. One day, she even gave Sariah a break and, with her girls, pulled Hannah around the village and let Hannah use their voices to tell them that her father was going to the temple to say a special prayer for her.

Most of the villagers had grown to love Hannah and her attentive parents. Some, however, still shunned the family, especially since Hannah's fits had started. People had told Joanna that they believed her to be possessed of demons when she would thrash about, but they said it only once. After the tongue-lashing Joanna gave them, they avoided her. It was apparent, though, by the way they turned away when Hannah was out in the village, that some still persisted in their beliefs.

Joanna guarded Sariah from their talk and kept that pain to herself as she had grown to love Hannah almost as fiercely as Sariah did.

On one particular day while Joanna walked Hannah around the village, she turned a corner and met Mariam face-to-face, just as she had years before. Mariam was a person Joanna avoided.

"Mariam, how are you?" Joanna asked politely, stopping the wagon suddenly. She stepped back unconsciously to shield Hannah from Mariam's curious gaze and pulled her daughters around her.

Mariam wasted no time on good manners. "I hear Joshua will be going with the others to Jerusalem," she said with a question in her voice.

"That's the plan," Joanna replied.

Mariam humphed in indignation. "What does he hope to accomplish? Is there a miracle waiting for him there? Perhaps a star?" she said with sarcasm.

"I don't know, Mariam. Surely their faith and humility will find a reward there."

Mariam looked at her narrowly.

"What is your interest in my family?" she asked.

Joanna returned her tone. "Your family? You call them your family, yet you treat them as outcasts."

Mariam rolled her eyes. "You don't understand. What should a person of faith do when a member of the family calls down a curse upon it?"

Joanna was shocked, although Mariam's revelation opened an understanding to her of why Mariam shunned her family.

"You think they are cursed from some bad deed?"

"Perhaps. That is for God to determine."

"And you speak for God?" Joanna asked. "I daresay God looks down on their devotion and service to their daughter with acceptance."

Mariam shook her head in disgust. "Then perhaps Joshua *will* bring home some miracle from the temple."

For several seconds that stretched in silence, the two women stared at each other until, finally, Joanna broke the stare.

"Come, girls," she said, pushing them in front of her, "let's go."

She whispered to Mariam as they passed. "The only curse this family has is you."

Mariam was speechless, and Joanna pulled the wagon by her, refusing to look at her eyes. When they were out of ear-shot, little Rachel said innocently, "I can't believe you said that."

Joanna stopped the wagon and faced the girls who stood with wide eyes before her. "Me neither," she answered with a grimace. She looked seriously down into her daughters' faces. "Make a vow that you will never tell Sariah what just happened. It would hurt her, and you don't want to hurt her, do you? It is not true. God does not curse people with crippled children. Do you understand? Will you promise?"

The girls solemnly nodded their heads.

"Good, now let's go home." She glanced back at Hannah to see that she had fallen asleep. Joanna hoped she had neither heard nor understood that exchange.

They wended their way back through the village. When they returned to Sariah's home, they found her asleep in the warm afternoon light, one hand still holding the needle and one the cloth.

The morning the temple journey began, all the people came out at the edge of the village to say good-bye to those who were to travel to Jerusalem. It was the same as the years before, but this time Joshua was going.

He had put on his new clothes earlier that morning, exclaiming over and over again how beautiful they were. He hugged his wife several times, thanking her for her gift. Although her fingers were sore from the hours of stitching, Sariah's heart was full of love for him and excitement for his trip.

They had pulled Hannah in her wagon so she could be part of the celebration. She squealed and waved her arms in joy as people bent over to speak to her. Sariah tried to count the people in the crowd but got confused after one hundred. It seemed to her there was no one in the village who did not come, and about half of those were going on the trip.

When it was almost time to go and the donkeys patiently stood waiting for those who would ride, Joshua swept Hannah into his arms and held her tight against his chest.

He whispered in her ear, "I go to the temple for you, my daughter. I will pray that God will bless you and bless us as we care for you." He kissed her on the cheek and gently laid her back down on her blankets.

Sariah's eyes filled with tears as he hugged her and then held her back so he could look into her face.

"Don't cry, Sariah, or else I won't go," he said, concern in his voice.

"They are tears of happiness for your journey," she said. "So don't think them tears of disappointment."

"Will you be all right?" he asked once more.

"I will be fine. Hannah will take care of me."

They both looked down at Hannah, who lay wide-eyed and still. Sariah smiled down at her in reassurance, and she smiled back.

"I'll be back within four days."

"You've told me that one hundred times," she said with a laugh.

"Have I told you a hundred times that I love you?"

"Only ninety-nine," she teased. "Tell me once more."

"I do love you," he said. He rubbed her cheek with his hand. Then he dropped his hand and clasped hers, as if reluctant to go.

The crowd jostled around them as the procession began to leave, but Joshua held on.

"Go, Joshua. We'll be fine," Sariah urged.

Kissing her quickly one more time, he picked up his bag, slung it over his shoulder, and walked away, his head turned to keep his eyes on his small family. He bumped into someone, quickly apologized, and then looked back to see Sariah holding up Hannah at her shoulders to watch her father leave. She was laughing at his clumsiness.

"I love you," he called back.

"And I you," Sariah said.

Then he turned and was swallowed up in the crowd.

Sariah knelt down beside Hannah and held her hand, pressing her lips against the fragile skin and thin bones. Her eyes filled with tears again.

"We'll be fine, won't we, Hannah?" she murmured, trying to summon courage she suddenly didn't feel.

Watching until the crowd disappeared over a small hill, she finally looked around to see they were the only two still peering at the horizon.

"Come, let's go home," she said. She stood up and feigned happiness. "We'll go and give our home a good cleaning so that all will be bright and sparkling when your father returns."

Without another look toward where the noisy pilgrimage could still be heard but not seen, she picked up the handles of the wagon and turned toward home, the thought of arriving there bringing her a deep sense of loneliness.

Hannah said, "Puh, puh," all the way home.

Sariah explained over and over to her on the trek home why her father had left in such a large crowd as her arms became as tired and aching as her heart was.

Finally, they reached home, and Sariah pulled Hannah in, the inside of the house dark and the day stretching out ahead endlessly.

10

More Despair for Sariah

Until she faced being without him for four days, Sariah hadn't realized how much she depended upon Joshua's visits throughout the day to give her a break in the never-ending task of caring for Hannah.

On the second day he was gone, and with one long day over, she decided she would take Hannah outside after they ate and before she napped.

Lifting Hannah off the floor proved even more difficult now that there was no one with strong arms to help her. She tried to speak brightly to Hannah, always diligent in her desire that Hannah not feel she was a burden.

Bending down from her waist, she lifted Hannah with her arms under her knees and shoulders. A now-familiar pain in her lower back became stronger as she began to lift.

"Here, my girl, let's go outside and feel the warmth of the sun," she struggled to say. "Perhaps we'll walk down and see what Joanna and her girls are doing today."

"Puh, puh," Hannah said. Sariah could hear a tremor of excitement in her voice.

"No, not yet," she answered, carrying Hannah over to her wagon parked beside the door. Although Hannah remained thin, almost skeletal during the weeks when the heat took away her appetite, she had grown a little longer. Her arms and legs couldn't control which way they moved as she was being carried, so it was a delicate task of holding on to her while her head, arms, and legs fought against being held tightly.

Sariah exhaled strongly as she laid Hannah down and then smiled at her.

"Your father will be home in two days," she said. At that, Hannah squealed in delight.

She was almost too long for the small wagon, which was becoming more rickety by the day.

"When your father comes home, he will have to make a new wagon for your long legs."

Sariah carefully tucked a pillow at the end of the wagon to protect Hannah's feet and then slowly pulled the wagon out of the door, blinking at the bright light of midday that peeked around the edges of the canopy. Hannah blinked also and moved her head back and forth. Sariah shielded her eyes with her own hands until Hannah could grow accustomed to being outside.

Not in the mood to sew, Sariah pulled her stool up beside Hannah and took her hand.

Hannah talked away, saying "Puh, Puh" over and over.

Sariah knew she tried in her own way to understand where her father was.

But as Sariah watched the lives playing out their dramas on the street before them, she hardly heard her. The few travelers passing through the narrow streets stirred up thick clouds of dust as they led their pack animals and laughed loudly among themselves. Down the street, children played a simple game with sticks—children who were born in the years after the slaughter, younger than Hannah but whose strong bodies had overtaken hers while they were still infants.

Young people, on a break from school, flirted and teased with each other in the streets, reminding Sariah of when it was she and Joshua leaning into each other, smiling and staring with deep, secret intent into each other's eyes.

Women carried water jugs down toward the well, sharing their thoughts with their friends and not even noticing the woman sitting beside the wagon at a tiny house. Others walked by with baskets of fruits from the village's small market.

Sariah had bought what she could before Joshua had left, knowing she would never be able to take Hannah in her wagon to the marketplace alone and pick out the day's meals among the jostling crowd.

On other days, Sariah would have called out and beckoned others to come to where she sat, asking them how their lives fared and what they were doing with the hours that day. This day, however, she sat lost in her thoughts, imagining what her life would have been like if the star had not given Hannah life, though it was only a shadow of a life.

Finally, Hannah's cries broke through Sariah's reverie. Jerking her head around, Sariah noticed flies had landed on Hannah's face. She quickly brushed them away.

"I am so sorry, Hannah. I was lost in my thoughts." She brought Hannah's hand to her lips. "The other people—they don't even see us, do they?" she asked regretfully.

Hannah answered for perhaps the hundredth time with "Puh, puh."

Without thinking, Sariah once again said, "Your father will be home in two days." She kissed Hannah's hand again. "It can't be soon enough for me."

Suddenly, she looked down at Hannah's hand, puzzlement, then dread striking her heart.

She tried to move her daughter's wrist back and forth, but it no longer moved. Hannah's hand remained bent at the wrist, resisting her mother's efforts to straighten it. She quickly picked up her other hand. It was not quite as bent as the other one, but it too resisted movement.

"Hannah, straighten your hand out," she said. Holding her own out straight, she showed Hannah what she wanted her to do.

Thinking it was a game, Hannah waved her arm stiffly and opened her mouth in excitement. Sariah grabbed her arm and gently tried to bend her wrist again but couldn't. It had been stiff before, but now it was immovable.

A wave of grief constricted her throat, then moved to her heart where it sat as a heavy, unwelcome, uninvited guest. Somehow Sariah knew in that moment that Hannah's wrists would never bend again. Whatever she had hoped Hannah would be able to learn to do with her hands would never happen. Although she didn't understand why it had happened, she knew that it had happened.

With her heart melting in a familiar ache, she pushed Hannah's arms down with difficulty and put them by her side, tucking a blanket tightly around them. Perhaps if Hannah could not see them for a moment or two, she could release them and they would be straight again. Perhaps then pain would let go of the icy grip it held on her heart.

Folding her own arms across her chest, Sariah curled into herself and shrank back against the wall of the house. She closed her eyes against the tears that coursed down her cheeks. Refusing, as always, to let Hannah see her cry, she squeezed her arms tightly until the physical pain of that pressure was greater than the rawness in her heart. She gritted her teeth until her jaws ached and her tears ceased.

Pushing her grief so deep inside that she didn't have to deal with it in the light of day, a routine that was as familiar as breathing to her, she used her sleeve to wipe her tears from her cheeks and forced a smile on her face. Only then did she look down again at Hannah, who, suspecting that something was not right, had laid as still as she could, her arms still under the blanket.

"Let's go in and sleep," Sariah said to her. "It's too hot outside for such a sweet daughter as you." She smiled weakly, but it was enough for Hannah to respond with her own smile.

Shooing more flies away, Sariah picked up the handle and carefully turned the wagon around, pulling it into the dark house.

Inside, with Hannah settled down, Sariah sank into her own bed and tearlessly succumbed to oblivion.

Outside in the yellow sunshine, the life of the village continued, and no one even noticed that the woman who had sat beside the wagon in front of the small house was no longer there.

Sariah woke a couple of hours later to knocking at the door.

"Sariah? Sariah, are you there?" Joanna called in a bright voice.

Confused at first, Sariah took several seconds to realize where she was. Hannah lay not far away, still asleep, her head turned and mouth open with drool glistening on her chin.

Resisting the urge to wipe it away, Sariah quietly struggled to her feet and stumbled to the door, careful not to disturb her daughter.

She opened the door as Joanna started to knock again. She blinked against the bright light.

"Sariah, what are doing?" Joanna said. "I thought you would never answer."

"I . . . I was asleep," she said, keeping the door open only a bit.

Joanna looked puzzled. "You don't look well . . . Is everything all right? Where is Hannah?"

"We're fine."

"Open the door and let me come in," Joanna said teasingly. "The children are playing, and I came to visit you."

"Please, no. We're fine."

Joanna gently pushed the door, and Sariah stepped back, unable to deliberately keep Joanna out.

Joanna stepped inside. "It's so dark in here. Where are your lamps?"

"We were sleeping. Hannah is still asleep."

"I can tell there is something wrong," Joanna said with persistence. "What is it? I wondered why I didn't see you yesterday, but Rachel was sick, and I didn't go out."

She looked around the dark room and, finding a lamp dimly lit, raised the wick to bring light to the room. Then, finding Hannah in her bed, Joanna walked over to gaze down at her. Hannah began to stir.

"Is Rachel well now?" Sariah asked.

"She's fine, but what of you?" Joanna walked back over to Sariah and, putting her face close to hers, said, "What's wrong?"

Sariah had to smile, even with her heavy heart. "You are persistent."

"I'm your friend and I know your heart," she answered. "Come, sit down, and we'll talk." She put her arm around Sariah's shoulders and pulled her over to sit down on a cushion at the table. "Do you miss Joshua? Is Hannah sick?"

Sariah tried to be brave, but then her lips began to quiver, and in a rush of emotions, she told Joanna of her discovery about Hannah's tight wrists that morning.

"I didn't think she would get worse," Sariah said, sobs shaking her body. "Isn't it enough she can't talk or walk? That she'll never marry and hold a baby of her own? Isn't enough that she throws herself into fits and is pale and exhausted afterward?"

Joanna had no answers. All she had were her arms that she readily wrapped around Sariah, holding her while she cried.

Finally, worn out, Sariah sat still as Joanna patted her hands.

"I don't have answers to your questions," Joanna said. She sighed deeply, searching for words to comfort her dear friend. "But I do know that Joshua will be home soon, and I believe he'll have hope for you. I don't know how I know, but I do."

A small voice interrupted with a "Muh, muh." Hannah was awake.

"I do miss Joshua," Sariah said with a sigh.

"Of course, you do. But . . ." Joanna stood up, excitement filling her voice. "I have an idea." She walked over to Hannah and bent down to her. "Would you like to come stay with us, Hannah, until your father returns?"

"We can't do that," Sariah said. "You have no room."

"There is always room for friends." She bent back down to Hannah. "Tell your mother you want to sleep at my house."

Hannah tried her best. She said "Muh, muh" louder and louder until at last Sariah was forced to laugh and go to her side.

"We will. We will, Hannah," she said with a deep sense of relief. She was grateful she wouldn't have to face the next two days alone.

Within a few minutes, giggling like young girls again, she and Joanna had packed up the belongings they needed around Hannah. With both of them pulling the burdened wagon, they walked two roads over to Joanna's home.

Hannah was quiet with seeming amazement at the possibilities before her. She had been outside in her wagon many times but never with their clothes and her nighttime blankets tucked around her.

Her quietness lasted only until they reached Joanna's home, and Joanna opened the door to the noise and laughter of her three girls.

"Help us, girls," she said. "We have guests." She and Sariah began to unload the wagon that they pulled close to the door of the house, which was only slightly larger than Sariah's.

The girls, always attentive to Hannah, danced about the wagon with what seemed to be a hundred questions about this new happening in their lives.

"Talk less and carry more," Joanna chided. "Take the pallets and make a bed fit for a queen." She smiled at Hannah, who laughed and moved deliriously.

"I can help you carry Hannah in," Joanna said.

That idea seemed much too exciting for Hannah and, as she swung her arms wildly in the air, she hit the side of the wagon, nicking her thinly-fleshed hand and drawing blood.

The sudden pain stopped her laughter, and her eyes widened and filled with tears.

Seeing what happened, Sariah grabbed her hand and covered it with kisses.

"It's not bad, Hannah," she said soothingly. "Be brave, and we'll take you inside where there's laughter." She wiped the blood off with the hem of her dress. "See, it's just a little scratch. Now lie still, and I'll carry you inside."

"I'll help," Joanna said as Sariah bent down to lift Hannah.

"I don't need help." She urged Hannah to try to be still and pulled her up with a tiny grunt.

"You are so strong." Joanna shook her head in amazement as she had done many times before.

"I must be," Sariah answered directly. She followed Joanna into the house, walking as quickly as she could before Hannah became too heavy.

The next two days were glorious ones for Sariah as her burden was lightened through the kind love of friends and Hannah glowed in the attention that was freely given her in Joanna's home.

The first night they were there, the girls danced and sang around Hannah as she lay on a soft pallet piled high with blankets. They held her arms and twirled under them, telling her she was the best dancer of all.

Hannah squealed and sang in a tuneless voice until she was so exhausted that, with a deep sigh, she grew silent and gazed at the life around her.

When the girls tired themselves, they lay down by her and quickly fell asleep. Sariah and Joanna sat together quietly, their hearts full at the happiness of their daughters.

When the night grew late, they picked up Joanna's girls

and tucked them into their beds. Kneeling down beside her, Sariah made sure only softness touched Hannah and bent to place a gentle kiss on her forehead as she lay relaxed and pretty in her sleep.

While Joanna began to make her preparations for the night, Sariah quietly slipped outside and climbed the stairs to the upper level of the house. There she knelt beneath the stars and thanked her God for the blessings of the day. Tears, no stranger to her face, coursed down her cheeks as she called the blessings of heaven down upon her husband and prayed that God would bring him back safely with hope for her.

When she finally arose, she gazed upon the sky, trying to will one star to shine more brightly than all the others and fill her heart with the faith she felt she so often lacked.

She thought she saw one star gleam but not sure, she sent a thought heavenward that the same stars would shine down on her husband and speak of her love to him.

The next morning, the girls continued their delightful play around Hannah. With scarves and what little jewelry the humble house held, they dressed her as a princess and waited upon her as only royal servants would. Then they anointed her the queen and surrounded her with their straw dolls. She beamed in their attention.

Tiring of play, they moved the furniture aside and squeezed the wagon in next to the table. Then they propped Hannah up so she could watch the preparations of a sweet cake with honey, raisins, and dates that had been zealously guarded for just such a special day.

Against the feeble protests of Sariah, who thought it would

make a mess, Rachel put the bowl by Hannah's side, placed the spoon in her tight hand, and helped her stir the batter. If only for a moment, Hannah became a cook.

After the noonday meal, they walked out in the country-side as the girls vied to help Sariah pull Hannah's wagon.

"Your girls are so good to Hannah," Sariah said to Joanna as they rested in the shade of a scrubby tree.

"They sense divinity within you," she replied. "You walk among miracles and don't even know it."

"No, I don't," Sariah answered with a quiet laugh. "At least, it is not the miracle that I want."

Joanna looked off into the distance. "Do those miracles exist in this day?" she wondered. "Where are the miracles when soldiers can come one night and rob your baby of his life?"

"Do you think of Jared often?" Sariah asked. "You do not speak of him much."

"No, but he is always here." Joanna touched the spot on her chest where her heart beat.

"Then what miracles do I walk among when pain is in the shadow of every breath?" Sariah asked.

"Hannah brings forth a love from those she meets."

Sariah considered that for a moment. "Perhaps. But your daughters are young and have their lives before them. I am getting old, and Hannah is getting heavy."

"That is why it is a miracle. You face the truth of every day and still find the strength to get up with the sunrise and live."

"What would you have me do? Leave her on the hills and let her die?" Sariah didn't say it unkindly, just matter-of-factly.

"That is the miracle. To you it is no choice—you accept the difficult way as the only way."

"It is the only way," Sariah said. "And I await whatever may come. I just want it to be good."

"That then is the miracle that blesses my life," Joanna said.

They fell silent in the warmth of the afternoon, each lost in thoughts that were too tender to share.

11

Joshua's Return

Although Sariah loved the time at Joanna's home, the anticipation of Joshua's homecoming overshadowed her reluctance to return to her own life. Joanna and her girls accompanied Sariah and Hannah home, with cakes and breads they had made tucked in around Hannah.

Hannah had protested when they put her in the wagon to return home, but Sariah had spoken to her of the joyous reunion she would have with her father and of the wonderful tales he would have to tell her of the temple and the glorious city of Jerusalem.

Returning to their own home had seemed sad, so Sariah had given in to Joanna's repeated invitations to stay until close to the time the men were expected home. Now that they were back, Joanna quickly helped Sariah tidy her home and prepare a meal while her girls once more entertained Hannah.

Soon it was evening, and a cry could be heard out on the street that the caravan was approaching the village.

Sariah's heart leapt at the thought of Joshua's return. It took her but a moment to put Hannah in her wagon, then she and Joanna walked as quickly as they could to where a crowd had gathered to see the first sight of the travelers.

Sariah pulled Hannah up to the front so she could be one of the first to see her father. Overcome with a happiness she did not usually feel, she hugged Joanna who stood beside her.

"Thank you for your kindness and that of your daughters," she said. "You made my daughter happy for just a little while. For that, I will always love you."

"The blessing was ours," Joanna said. "We'll do it again. We'll send our husbands off for another trip."

"I don't think so," Hannah said with a laugh.

"Look, there he is now," Joanna said, pointing to the dusty travelers who were just appearing over the small hill. "Hannah, there's your father."

Hannah strained to look from where she was lying. Sariah, torn between running to Joshua and holding Hannah up, hesitated only a moment before bending over and lifting up Hannah's head and shoulders so she could see him.

With a loud shout, Joshua spied his daughter and wife and ran toward them, leaving the crowd behind him.

Sariah gently laid Hannah back and, unable to hold herself back any longer, ran to meet her husband.

He grabbed her up and whirled her around before putting her down and covering her face with kisses.

"I have missed you so," he said. "I thought about you so often it almost seemed like you were there. I have much to tell you." He pressed his lips on hers in a long kiss until she protested.

"Everyone is looking at us," she said.

"I don't care." Picking up his pack, he walked with his arm around her until they reached their daughter.

Hannah squealed with excitement at the sight and touch

of her father, who easily picked her up in his strong arms and whirled her around.

"Be careful, be careful," Sariah urged, laughing nonetheless.

"I wouldn't hurt Hannah," he assured her. He laid her back down and, kneeling beside her, stroked her hair with his hand. "I brought you a beautiful gift." He kissed her on the top of her head, then, standing up, placed his pack carefully beside her and picked up the handle of the wagon.

"Let's go home," he said. "I'm tired."

She hugged his arm and sighed. "Everything is much easier with you beside me."

"Was it too hard to care for Hannah?" he asked. They slowly walked toward home, the sounds of the reuniting villagers behind them. "I prayed you would have the strength."

She told him of the past two days and the care Joanna had given them.

"My prayers were answered then," he said.

When they reached their home, Sariah offered him the treats that Hannah had helped make, and he thanked his beaming daughter for his gifts.

Unexpectedly, he turned to Sariah and grabbed her arms with both his hands. His eyes were bright and his face flushed.

"When Hannah is asleep, we'll go sit under the stars, and I'll tell you of my trip," he said excitedly. "I believe I did bring you the good news you wanted."

"What? What did you see?" she said. "Tell me now."

"No, it will wait. The time must be right."

Intrigued, she took his bag as he picked up Hannah, carried her inside, and laid her down. She followed him in and started to beg him to tell her right then, but he placed a finger on her lips and said, "It will wait."

Removing his finger, he said, "Hush" when she started to speak again. Then he covered her lips with his kisses until the thoughts of what he might tell her were pushed back by the wonderful joy of having her husband home again.

Later, as the sun was setting and after Hannah had fallen asleep, Joshua took Sariah's hand and pulled her gently toward the stairs outside.

"But Hannah . . ." she protested.

"She's a sound sleeper. Come, we have to talk."

They walked up the stairs to the top floor and stood, looking out on the last pink that was adding a tint to the sky behind the hill. Then Joshua sat down with his back to the chimney and drew Sariah down close to him. Sitting quietly for a few minutes, they basked in the wonderful feeling of being together again.

Suddenly, he turned to Sariah and pulling away, he knelt before her, both her hands clasped tightly in both of his. His eyes were bright with excitement.

"I think I saw the savior," he said.

"The savior?" she asked incredulously.

"Yes, the savior, the child who was born the same night as our Hannah," he said. "The one who will save Israel."

She could not imagine such a thing.

"But didn't he die?" she asked wonderingly.

"I don't know how he didn't, but, Sariah, if he is God's savior, then God's angels would have protected him somehow. They protected Hannah, didn't they?"

"Yes," she said. "But how . . . how do you know he was the savior? Where did you see this child?"

He began to relate a tale whose very retelling made his eyes grow intense and his hands shake.

"It was yesterday as we packed up to leave the temple," he said. "There was a tremendous crowd of people, pushing this way and that, each vying for their own place. There were so many people, Sariah, that it was hard to breathe. But suddenly, the crowd parted, and a man and woman walked through, shouting with hoarse throats, asking if anyone had seen their son, a twelve-year-old boy they called 'Jesus.' They had not seen him for three days of their journey and had returned to find him."

"Missing three days? I can't imagine." She placed her hand over her heart.

He grabbed her hand back, as if anxious to draw her into the scene he was describing.

"I knew I had to help, so I followed the couple. By that time, I could see them only by the parting of the crowd. But suddenly a man at the top of the temple stairs called out. He said the child was inside. I pushed my way through, and then I saw them at the top of the stairs. The mother was sobbing."

He was silent for a moment, thinking, searching for an explanation.

"I don't know how I got to the top of the stairs. It was as if angels carried me above the crowd. I was suddenly so close I could almost touch them, and I followed them. It seemed like the crowd disappeared before me. Then I was there at the door, and there he was."

He bowed his head at the memory, and Sariah reached out to stroke his hair. Tears streamed down her face at his emotion.

"Go on," she gently urged. "What did he look like?"

Joshua looked up and continued, a faraway look now in his eyes.

"He was sitting on a high stool with the elders of the temple around him. They listened as he spoke. Their eyes never left his face. And his face was . . . pure and filled with light. His very voice pierced my heart. I cannot recall what he said, but it bore into my soul. A quiet feeling testified to me he was the boy I sought."

He was silent then as Sariah patiently waited for him to speak again.

He finally shook himself from his reverie and looked back into Sariah's eyes. The lowing of sheep and the sounds of the village settling down for the night were their background music.

"It was only a brief moment because his parents pushed through the crowds and gathered him in their arms," he continued softly. "I could not hear what his mother said, but he stood tall and said kindly, 'I would be about my father's business.'"

Sariah was puzzled.

"What did he mean? His father was searching for him."

"I do not know. Then he was gone. They disappeared from my sight, and I do not know how. As suddenly as I had found myself at the top of the stairs, it seemed I was at the bottom."

Trouble then clouded his face.

"I'm so sorry," he said. He took her hand and opened it, planting a kiss in the palm. "I couldn't find them again. I searched until dark, but I couldn't find them in the crowd. I asked people, but none knew who they were, except for one teacher who said he thought they traveled from the north. He said the boy had taught them much doctrine as if he had the authority from God."

Joshua bowed his head before Sariah. "I tried. I tried."

They said nothing for a minute as despair racked Joshua and Sariah pondered what he had told her. Then she wrapped him in her arms.

"There is nothing to be sad about," she said. "If he is the savior, we will find him again. If he is to save Israel, he will. If he will make Hannah well, he will. It is a wonderful thing to happen, Joshua. My faith is made stronger. We'll find him. God will help us."

He looked up at her and smiled. She wiped away his tears with her soft fingers.

"God showed him to you, and God will lead us to him," she said. "Your faith will be strong again."

Joshua reached out and pulled her in to him. "You are a good woman, Sariah. God will bless you for that."

"What did his mother look like?" she asked.

"She was beautiful and good," he said. "She looked a lot like you."

She laughed softly. "Perhaps years ago I was beautiful. Now I feel I am only tired."

He held her face between his hands. "You will always be beautiful to me. Every line on your face means but one day of goodness you have lived in service to my daughter and me."

He kissed her gently.

"I'll find the savior again. I will go to Jerusalem next year, and I will find him again."

"But what will he do for us, Joshua? Can he make Hannah walk or talk? If the savior would save Israel, how would that help Hannah? We seek for the savior, but do we know how he can help us?" Such questions had crowded her mind through the years, even as she had hoped.

Joshua shrugged his shoulders. "I don't know, but we must believe. His star shone down on her and brought her life. God saved her the night of the slaughter. Surely he has a plan for her. Can you believe that?" His eyes searched hers until she could no longer stand his gaze and looked down into her lap.

"I can try, but . . ." She wrenched her hands together, then slowly looked up again at her husband. Her chin quivered, and tears filled her eyes once more. "Hannah is getting worse, Joshua."

He protested. "No, she is not. She looks good."

Haltingly, Sariah told him of her discovery of Hannah's hands and how they could not bend at the wrist anymore. He held her as she cried and then hugged her tightly as she told him of the wonderful days she had spent at Joanna's house and how they had ministered to her and Hannah.

Eventually, her tears turned to smiles as she spoke of the girls' dances around Hannah and how Hannah had helped to make the cakes.

He held her back and looked directly at her. "See, there is a reason for faith. God saw your need and heard your prayers— before they even became words. He brought Joanna to you, and you were healed of your sorrow."

"Perhaps. But Hannah's hands still are bent."

His eyes were sad. "But your heart is better. Who can know the ways of God?"

She thought for a moment, unwilling to say words that would weaken his faith.

Finally, she said, "You are right, Joshua."

Just as she said that and turned her gaze upward again, a shooting star fell across the sky.

They both looked at it in wonder, then embraced each other with joyous laughter.

"God has spoken," Joshua said.

In her silence, Sariah agreed.

12

A Special Friend

There were no more falling stars as the years passed, however, and Hannah turned twenty-one, still as dependent on her parents' care as a newborn. In the homes around her, girls only slightly younger than Hannah grew up tender and beautiful, and the rituals of life and love were played out between them and the young men who had grown strong and handsome. In the marketplace, in the synagogue, in the streets on the warm evenings, Sariah watched and ached as life and its passages ignored her daughter.

Life remained unchanged for Sariah, who was now thirty-nine years old. Day after day became week after week, month after month, and year after year. The only change was that her days became ever more difficult as Hannah became heavier and tighter. Her wrists were now locked so that her fingers almost touched her forearms. The same tightness drew her ankles in and crossed her legs over each other unless Sariah put a rolled up blanket between them. Her toes folded and bent into each other.

Her hair was still shiny and sleek, and Sariah spent each

night brushing it out around her as she spoke to Hannah of queens in far-off lands whose hair could not compare to her princess's. One afternoon each week, Sariah heated the water Joshua had brought from the well the night before and, kneeling down at Hannah's head, washed her hair and rinsed it with water that smelled of perfumes Sariah had purchased with her sewing money.

Hannah's fits of shaking and trembling came at least twice weekly, but Sariah was no longer as frightened by them. She sat by Hannah's side and bathed her face with a cloth or held her head tightly when the fits were the worst so that Hannah could not gnash her tongue and her lips with her grinding teeth. When she finished, sometimes after one fit, sometimes after many, Sariah was limp with exhaustion also and grateful that Hannah would sleep. After many years of those difficult days, Sariah would no longer take the time while Hannah slept to tidy her home and prepare dinner. She just crawled over to her own bed and, pulling the covers over her head, fell into her own restless sleep. When Joshua came home at the end of the day and found them both asleep, he knew how the afternoon had been and quietly watched over them until they awoke, often with his head in his hands, wondering and praying about what he could do to help his small family.

Sariah continued to sew daily when Hannah felt well. She could only sew in the sunlight as her eyes had grown older and weak with the strain. Her stitches remained straight and small, though, and the traders who made their way through the small village brought her beautiful fabric that she carefully worked into well-made clothes for them to pick up on their way back the next few months.

Sariah's back had begun to curve from bending over her sewing and the constant strain of picking up Hannah and moving her this way and that to find a comfortable spot for her. Each year also grew more difficult for Hannah to live without pain.

As her limbs grew tighter, she often whimpered from the stretched muscles. At her cries, Sariah and Joshua warmed damp cloths by the fire and put them over her legs and arms with herbs that promised relief. Hannah smiled up at them, and they would feel new energy, if only for a moment, in caring for her.

Although Hannah remained small, Joshua had made her a larger wagon so she could continue to lie close by as Sariah sat outside, talking to Hannah in mindless repetition as she watched the lives of those around her with a humble envy. Through the long hours, she daydreamed of a life where it was Hannah who was bringing home a handsome man for them to meet and the sewing in Sariah's hands was a lovely wedding robe for her daughter.

Always, every day, Sariah sought for news of the savior until even her friends dismissed her with curt, yet polite, replies. Joshua returned every year to the temple in Jerusalem at Passover but never again saw the family who had lost their son and found him in the temple teaching.

Before each trip, Joshua begged Sariah to take the journey with him and Joanna offered to care for Hannah, but after so many years of her small world and the safety of the village, Sariah found herself unable to take such a long trip. Joshua continued to ask, however, and reassure her until Sariah trembled with indecision and cried, then he would hold her and tell her he understood and that he would go for them.

But Sariah continued to ask every visitor to the village if they knew of any young man who seemed as if he could be the savior. Most didn't even understand what she was talking about, but Ishmael had become a special friend as he traveled yearly through the country and always regarded her questions with patience. He made sure to pay her a generous amount of coins for the sewing he ordered each year from her.

Through the years, Ishmael had grown older and fatter, the number of his chins almost as many as the rings and bracelets on his fingers. Although his sons now stood at the head of his business, Ishmael still traveled high atop a camel with their caravan and insisted their yearly journeys take them through the village where Hannah lived. Leaving his caravan at the marketplace, he would lumber down through the streets to visit Sariah and Hannah, a servant or two behind with gifts.

At the sight of the merchant making his way toward them one day, Sariah stood up from her sewing stool with excitement. Hannah, who was lying beside her, widened her eyes as she saw her friend approach. She squealed and laughed and reached out as best she could to welcome him, struggling to mouth "Ish, Ish," one of the few words she could say.

"My daughters, my daughters, my beautiful daughters," he said with a thunderous voice, enveloping Sariah in such a hug that she could not breathe, much less speak.

Letting her go, he leaned over Hannah and, taking her head in his chubby hands, bent over with difficulty to plant a kiss on her forehead.

"You are still the most beautiful girl I see in all my travels," he told her. "You alone remain ageless, while all the others turn to wrinkles and bags."

The attention brought a smile to Hannah.

"And you . . ." He turned to Sariah. "You are still beautiful, although you could use some flesh on your bones." He pinched her cheek. "You are much thinner than last year, my child."

She smiled. "And much more tired also."

Ishmael snapped his fingers at his servant, who came bowing and bending before Sariah. He held a large package before her, which she reluctantly took.

"Here are some wonderful cakes from Jerusalem and the best fruits I could find," he said. "You must make our lovely Hannah a special meal and . . ." he nodded at Sariah, "you must eat a generous amount yourself."

"I can't take this," Sariah said. "There are others with less than we have. God has richly blessed us."

He wrapped her in a hug again, motioning with his hand for the servant to take the gifts inside.

"No one refuses the gifts of Ishmael," he said, releasing her. He turned once more to Hannah. "Do you want a cake for supper, Hannah?"

She answered with another squeal and more shaking of her arms.

"There. It is decided," he said, and Sariah knew not to argue.

"May I?" he asked, pointing to the stool.

"Always, Ishmael. Your goodness makes you a king in our home."

Lowering himself with a grunt, he snapped his fingers at the other servant, who produced a bolt of rich material with stripes of many colors from a bag.

"I have an order for you," Ishmael said. "I desire a sash to go around my more-than-ample waist, which I will pick up months from now. From whatever is left, I want you to make our Hannah a beautiful dress in which she will glow brighter than any star in the sky."

Sariah protested. "This is too much material." She couldn't help fingering the cloth, almost reverently. "It will just take a little bit for a sash, and that will leave much more than I need for a dress for Hannah."

"Good. Make yourself one also." He gestured again, and the servant disappeared into the house.

Sariah smiled. "You are too good to us."

"It's nothing," he said. "There is always more cloth." He moved his stool closer to Hannah. "Let me tell you the tales of my travels while my sons haggle in the marketplace and make eyes at the beautiful girls."

Sariah leaned against the wagon and wiped Hannah's mouth as Ishmael told them of places she could hardly imagine. Hannah listened wide-eyed, and neighbors, familiar with the sight of Ishmael, stopped and gathered around to share in his stories.

After an hour, as Ishmael continued with no end in sight, a servant came down the street to summon him for his sons.

"Alas, I must go and leave my friends." He struggled to his feet as the neighbors went on their way. Left alone with Sariah and Hannah, he bent down once more to kiss Hannah. "You be well," he said. "When I return, I want to see you in your dress."

He turned to Sariah and clasped her hands in his. "Take care, my child."

She looked at him with questioning eyes. "Ishmael . . ." she began hesitantly.

"What? What do you desire of me? You know it is yours." He swept his arm before her as if the world were his to give.

"May I ask you—in all your travels, have you met a man of Hannah's age who seems a savior? Who seems more like a teacher when he is of the age to be the student?"

"Ahh, the savior you have asked about before," Ishmael said slowly. "The savior the children of Israel have looked for since ancient times?" He looked into her face but wasn't mocking her.

She waited expectantly as he thoughtfully put one finger on the side of his plump cheek and narrowed his eyes in thought.

"I don't know of anyone who will save Israel from their oppressors," he said, "but . . . now that you remind me . . ."

"What?" She held her breath.

"A man traveled with us for a while who spoke of a young man in his village who seemed wise beyond his years, who spoke of the mysteries of God as if they were no mysteries at all." He shrugged his shoulders. "But that is all. He was from the north, perhaps, as I remember."

Sariah could hardly contain her excitement; she grabbed his arm. "That's him. I know it. He is the one whose star brought life to Hannah."

Ishmael clucked his tongue. "You may believe, dear child, but I hardly think a man of such a modest village could save Israel. Has anything good ever come of Nazareth?"

"Nazareth," she said, her hopes suddenly dashed. "It is so far away. How will I find him? How will I get there?"

"Why do you need to find him?" Ishmael asked.

Sariah had never shared the story of Hannah's birth with Ishmael, but looking into his kind eyes, she knew he would understand. "He will help Hannah. I know. I have waited for so long since the night his star gave Hannah life."

She told him the story of that night and how long she had sought the savior and how Joshua had seen the young man at the temple. Ishmael responded to her with sympathy, putting his hand on her shoulder at the end of it and nodding his head.

"No one could deny you or Hannah any wish of your heart," he said. "I will try to find him for you. You stay here and care for your daughter, and I will bring word of him when I return in several months."

"You will?" She clasped her hands in delight. "I can wait. And I will pray each night that you will be led to the savior." She hugged him as tightly as she could. "Thank you, Ishmael."

"No," he said. "Thank you for your faith."

After another hug and a tender caress of Hannah's soft hair, Ishmael slowly made his way down the street.

As he disappeared, Sariah waved Hannah's arm with her own and said, "Hannah, when our friend returns, he will bring good news. I know it."

Later that night, Sariah talked endlessly about her visit with Ishmael to Joshua. It was unusual to him to see her so animated, but when she finally grew weary of talking and sat at the table smoothing the beautiful fabric Ishmael had brought her, he walked over from where he had been standing by the fire.

He pulled her back into him, his strong arms around her.

"Nazareth is a long way away," he said.

She reached up and patted his arm. "It will be all right. I don't know how, but it will be."

He buried his face in her hair. "I hope so, Sariah. I hope so." He sighed. "But . . . but don't be sad if our life is never more than it is now. I have you, and I have Hannah, and that is enough for me."

She stood up, and he quickly let her go as she turned to face him, an unusual fire in her eyes.

"My life is hard, my pain is real," she said sharply. "Hannah only gets worse. Do not take this hope from me." Tears filled her eyes. "You don't have to stay here day after day and do the same tasks over and over with her never getting any better. This is not the life I thought mine would be. Why have you stopped believing?"

He placed his hands gently on either side of her face. "I haven't stopped. I'm sorry. It's just been so long, and I do not want to see you heartbroken." He hesitated. "You are right. I will join you once again in believing. If Ishmael returns and tells you of this man that knows God, we'll find him."

She looked down. "But it's so far away."

"Now you are telling me not to have faith?" he chided her gently.

"Never," she said, looking back up with a smile.

"Good."

She covered his lips with hers, then pulled away. "Now I will begin the most glorious sash Ishmael has ever worn." She chuckled. "It will be the longest one I have ever made."

The joy he had snatched away returned, and she picked up her fabric. He looked at her silently for a long minute, then turned away to his own tasks.

13

A Special Gift

Several months later, Sariah had finished Ishmael's sash with every stitch small and perfect. She carefully cut out the generous amount of fabric left and crafted a dress, speaking to Hannah as she did it of what a beauty she would be and how Ishmael would bring them wonderful news as he looked upon Hannah in her lovely dress.

With the cloth that was left, she made herself a pillow she could clasp closely to her at night and fall asleep with a prayer on her lips that Ishmael would soon come back to them with the good news she yearned for.

Joshua never again said a word that cast a shadow upon her dreams, even when the months turned into a year and then still more without the return of Ishmael.

When it was six months past the time Ishmael would have returned for the year, Sariah spoke quietly to Joshua, her words coming slowly. "I don't know why Ishmael hasn't come."

"If it's within his power, he'll be here," Joshua said. "He is an old man. Perhaps he has been sick."

"Perhaps." She didn't say much more, but she did not sleep

with the pillow that night or any night after.

At the end of summer, Rachel became betrothed to a smart young man from a nearby village where they would move once they were married.

"You will make Rachel's dress, won't you?" Joanna asked one evening as she and Sariah carried water from the well. It was Sariah's favorite time of the day—she could be out in the fresh air and, just for a moment, pretend her life was normal.

"Of course," she replied. Then quietly, she said, "Perhaps Rachel could just wear Hannah's dress of Ishmael's material. It is beautiful, and I don't think he's coming again to see us."

"He'll be back when he can," Joanna said, taking her friend's hand. "But Hannah will wear her dress at Rachel's wedding. She will come and laugh, and we'll make her feel as though she is the beautiful bride."

"I try not to live in dreams," Sariah said sadly. "The awakening is too hard."

Joanna squeezed her hand hard. "We will try just for one night to believe life is all we wish it could be. Please, Sariah, can we?"

Sariah looked at her friend, wishing that she had not brought sadness to the conversation.

"You know I would never do anything to take from Rachel's joy. Of course we'll believe," she said.

They continued their walk with Joanna babbling on about her daughter's wedding plans and Sariah trying very hard not to covet her happiness.

Over the next four months, Sariah worked diligently to make Rachel's dress the most exquisite that had ever been seen in the village. The joy and excitement of Rachel and her family was contagious, and Sariah was able to join in their happiness, even when she knew Joanna's joy at the marriage of her daughter would never be hers. Sariah thanked God each night during that time that Hannah in her limited understanding was not aware of how different and narrow her life was. To Sariah alone, and Joshua to a lesser extent, was left that pain.

Soon it was the first night of the wedding celebration, and all the village rejoiced with Rachel's family. The night was blessedly warm, and Sariah spent much time dressing Hannah, whose stiffness defied ease in putting on the dress her mother had sewn. When that task was finished and Sariah's energy almost spent, she sang songs to Hannah, brushing out her hair and twisting it into long braids intertwined with ribbons.

"Now, don't drool," she said to Hannah as Joshua placed her in her wagon. "You don't want to get your dress wet. You are so lovely."

Yet, knowing her chin would not stay dry long, she tucked a towel beside her.

Joshua stepped back and looked at the two girls he loved. "You both rival the stars in their beauty."

"And your eyesight is becoming dim," Sariah said, slapping him playfully on the chest. His hair had grown gray around the edges, and lines framed his face, but his eyes were still bright with love when he looked at his wife.

Her hair was mostly gray, and creases lined her mouth and eyes, but when she pulled her hair back and smiled up at him, she felt like the young girl he had married so long before.

"If I'm old, you're only a few years behind," he said. Turning to Hannah, he winked. "I think your mother is as beautiful as you. What do you think?" She struggled to nod her head in agreement, bringing a gentle smile to his lips.

"Let's go eat and drink and laugh," he said. He took up the handles of the wagon, and they made their way to Joanna and Simon's happy home where the villagers had gathered. Pulling the wagon close to the house, they propped her up as best they could that she might see the celebration before her. Joanna brought stools from the house, and they sat on both sides of Hannah, including her in the conversation as they spoke to the people celebrating around them.

For once, which Sariah deemed an answer to prayer, she did not feel sorrow as she sat beside Hannah and watched her eyes sparkle as others her age danced and sang. People of the village who had been kind to Hannah through the years brought warmth to Sariah's soul as they came to stand by Hannah and tell her how pretty she looked. With each compliment, Hannah shook her arms in her attempt to dance and join in. Some friends even held onto her arms and shook them rhythmically to the music. As always, Sariah appreciated their attempts to include Hannah.

Sariah and Joshua had not seen Mariam much in the past years since she had turned her back on their needs. They didn't know whether she was embarrassed or frustrated at their refusal to deny their daughter. But that evening, she was there, and they saw her stand as far away as possible from them and turn her back each time they looked in her direction.

"It doesn't matter," Joshua said to Sariah when he saw her glance toward her aunt and then drop her gaze to her hands folded in her lap. "She is the one who has refused the blessings of knowing us and Hannah."

Sariah knew that in her mind, although it was hard to believe it in her heart.

As the evening drew on and the revelers became even noisier, Sariah turned to Joshua. "I think Hannah is tired. We should go home." Hannah had grown more still, jerking when she began to doze, until finally she lay expressionless, smiling only when someone spoke to her and roused her from her sleepiness.

"It has been a long evening," Joshua said. He bent to tuck the blankets around Hannah for her ride home as the sun barely peeked over the hills.

From the corner of her eye, Sariah saw a man push his way through the crowd and suddenly appear at her side, where he bowed deeply.

Her heart leapt within her.

"Are you not one of Ishmael's?" she asked. She clutched Joshua's arm in a silent plea for support at whatever news would bring his servant and not Ishmael.

"I am. I have brought you word from Ishmael." He bowed again.

Sariah scanned the crowd. "Is he here? Where has he been these many months?"

The crowd continued its celebration, and only the couple could hear his reply. Joshua grabbed a nearby lantern and held it so they could see his face.

"I, Hassan, have returned to give you word of Ishmael's death," the servant said solemnly.

Sorrow sliced through Sariah's heart and made her weak-kneed. It was what she had feared in her darkest moments of doubt. Joshua put an arm around her and steadied her as she cried out. "Tell me it is not so. I made his sash. I made Hannah's dress. See? Doesn't she look beautiful? He was to return with a message. Where is he?"

Joshua held her tighter and shushed her as her voice edged on hysteria.

"His sons travel to a nearby village and have sent me here

to deliver a message to you as their father insisted," Hassan said, bowing once more before her.

But Sariah had her face buried in her hands.

"Tell us," Joshua said.

"Ishmael died last year—about the time he was to return here. He died a gentle death, worthy of the kind man he was. Before he died, he gave one son a message to tell to the sweet mother who attends her daughter in this village."

At that, Sariah looked up, a glimmer of hope returning. She began to shake with expectation.

"Did he find the savior?" she asked.

Hassan looked puzzled. "I know of no savior, but this was his message. He said, 'The man you seek abides in Nazareth.'" He spoke it as if he had practiced many times. "I am sorry, but I do not know of whom he speaks."

"I do, I do," Sariah said. The depth of her joy was now equal to that of her despair moments before. "The savior. He spoke of the savior. Is that all? What more did he say?" She clutched at his sleeve while he patiently looked into her eyes as Ishmael once had.

"His son said Ishmael left you a gift to help you in your search."

It was now Sariah's turn to look bewildered. "A gift? I don't need a gift. I only need to know where the savior lives."

A smile played about Hassan's mouth, and his eyes glittered in the lamplight. "Perhaps you will want this."

From his robe he pulled a necklace, a heavy gold chain with a large oval purple stone suspended from it. Gasping at its beauty, Sariah recognized it as one of the jewels Ishmael always wore.

"It is yours," Hassan said, holding the necklace out to her.

But she stepped back from his offering.

"I can't take it," she said. "I could never wish for something so beautiful."

"Ishmael said to take this necklace and use it to find for whom you search." He held it out again in front of her.

But Sariah still stayed back. She looked up to Joshua.

"Take it, Sariah," Joshua said. "It is yours. Ishmael wanted you to have it."

She clasped her hands at her chest. "But what do I want of it? I want only word of the savior."

"Perhaps this will help you get to him," Hassan said. "Much can be bought for a price." He handed the jewel to Joshua and bowed again. "May the blessings of the house of Ishmael be upon you."

Turning on his heel, he disappeared into the crowd. Several people close to the couple had seen Ishmael's gift and now stood whispering behind their hands to each other.

Joshua tucked the necklace inside his cloak. He and Sariah looked at each other for the briefest of moments, not knowing what to say.

Sariah finally spoke. "He is right, my husband. When God could not send Ishmael, he opened another way for us to find the savior. Such are the ways of God."

"Perhaps," Joshua said. He placed his hand on Sariah's back and gently nudged her toward where Hannah now slept. "Come, let's go home before our good fortune becomes the cause for this night's celebration."

14

A Good-bye

Word of the beautiful jewel Joshua and Sariah had received as a gift spread throughout the village, and in the beginning, people would cautiously knock on their door and ask to see the necklace. Joshua and Sariah politely refused all but their closest friends, keeping the jewel hidden behind a heavy stone in the fireplace.

Soon, however, the people forgot, and life returned to normal in the never-ending care of Hannah.

But for Joshua and Sariah the knowledge of the necklace was always before them, and each evening they spoke of its possibilities, for Joshua had joined his wife in believing that perhaps they could find the savior. During the following weeks and eventually months, a plan began to form in the couple's thoughts.

"We can sell the jewel and buy a wagon and donkey for the journey to Nazareth," Joshua said. "It will be a long and hard journey for Hannah, but if God wants us to do it, I believe he'll prepare a way for us to accomplish it."

"Perhaps the savior will want the jewel, though. Maybe we shouldn't sell it," Sariah said.

"If he's of God, I doubt that's his way," Joshua said, "but perhaps."

"If you go and take the jewel to him, maybe he will come to us," Sariah said, dreading above all a journey that would tax the strength of their frail daughter.

"Perhaps." He patted her hand.

Then, as in other nights, conversation turned quiet, and each was left with thoughtful, silent hopes.

And so they lived a life marked by "perhaps" until summer turned to fall and then to winter, and they decided to buy a wagon and a donkey for a journey in the spring if Hannah's health permitted. If they determined she couldn't make the trip, Joshua would go. Sariah did not know which she wished for least—the long trial of traveling with Hannah or the long days and evenings of being without Joshua.

That winter, which was chillier than usual, Hannah's fits increased, and most days left her without energy, lying pale and weak as her parents urged her to eat and to drink warm milk to build up her strength. Some days she ate, others she did not. She grew even thinner.

After Joshua came home from work one day with a deep cough and aching head, Hannah fell sick the next day. She lay on her bed, her eyes glassy, shaking first with chills and then fever. Sariah wrapped her in blankets warmed by the fire when she was cold, then wiped her forehead with cool cloths when she was hot. She held her for hours on end, either sitting or kneeling beside her, mindlessly crooning the songs of her childhood. When Hannah's body was wracked with coughing, she held her up, praying that her daughter would catch her

breath. Her own relief came when Hannah would finally suc-
cumb to a restless sleep and Sariah would lie down beside her,
her arm over her, and quickly fall asleep herself.

The first three or four days, Joanna stopped by, bringing
food to tempt Hannah, but soon her household was struck with
the illness, and she stayed home to nurse her own family.

Sariah escaped the sickness that threatened so many in the
village. Whether that was a blessing or a curse, she couldn't
decide. After hours of tending Hannah day and night, she
yearned for the comfort of her own bed and uninterrupted
sleep.

Joshua struggled to work until one day, coming home
early, he stood and looked down at his sick daughter and tired
wife.

"Is she worse?" he asked, coughing long and deep himself.

"She's no better." Sariah took her eyes from Hannah's face
and moved to relieve her back from its soreness. Looking up at
her husband, she was shocked at his appearance.

Dark circles under his eyes made his pale face look almost
white, his cheeks bright with fever. He hugged his arms to his
chest and struggled to breathe.

"Joshua, you are so much sicker," Sariah said. She gently
laid Hannah down, covered her up, and rose with stiff limbs to
face her husband.

Pressing her hand against his forehead, she drew back from
its fire.

"You have to lie down." She put her arm around him to
guide him to the bed, but he resisted.

"No, I came home early to help with Hannah. You're so
tired." Coughs wracked him again, and he bent over, struggling to regain his breath.

"I am tired but not sick," she said, leading him over to the bed where she tucked him in.

Straining with the weight, she pulled Hannah's bed over beside Joshua's and laid down between them, her fear of becoming sick herself replaced with fear of them becoming worse.

For the next two days, Joshua trembled, delirious with a fever.

"Please, God, give me strength" was the constant prayer on Sariah's lips and in her heart.

During the daylight hours, she spooned a thin soup into their mouths and at night, dipped water for them that had been left outside the door to cool. A physician from a neighboring village came to theirs, making his rounds to each home where the sickness hovered. He gave Sariah herbs to add to the soup.

"It will run its course, and they will be well like the others," he assured her.

Looking down at the weak shadows of her husband and daughter, she found it hard to believe.

"Don't forget to take care of yourself," he said, gently putting his hand on her shoulder. "You are so thin."

She tried. When both Joshua and Hannah happened to sleep at the same time, she sat before the fire, trying to get warm and to eat the bread and fruit one of Joanna's daughters had brought. Her fear choked her, though, and she put the food aside, instead forcing down a cup of juice and gagging on its sweetness.

As the evening of the fourth day came, Sariah added a few vegetables to the pot of soup on the fire and took down one of the cloths that had been drying on the hearth. She had bent to dip it into the jug and bathe them once more when she heard a weak sound.

From her bed, Hannah called, "Muh, muh."

It was the song of heavenly angels to Sariah, and she rushed to her daughter's side and knelt down beside her.

"What did you say, Hannah?" She put her hands on both Hannah's cheeks and found them cool to the touch. Her fever had broken.

"Oh, Hannah, you are better." She gathered her into her arms.

"Puh, puh," she said, smiling weakly.

"Your father is still sick," Sariah replied. She turned Hannah's head so she could see her father lying not far from her, then laid her back down. Reaching over the bed, Sariah gently touched Joshua. "Joshua, Hannah is better. Her fever has broken."

Joshua half-opened his eyes but showed no sign that he heard or saw Sariah.

"Hannah is better, Joshua, so I know you'll feel better soon too." She turned Hannah's head back so as not to frighten her with the sight of her sick father.

While Joshua thrashed about, Sariah struggled once more to pull Hannah in her bed over to the side of the room. She spent the rest of the evening bathing and changing Hannah into fresh clothes and combing out the tangles of her hair. Sitting beside her for more than an hour, she persuaded Hannah to eat a bowl of soup with promises of walks in the sunshine and visits to Joanna's house.

But worry for Joshua battled against her happiness that Hannah was better. His moans interrupted her conversations with her daughter.

When Hannah finally slept again, Sariah covered her and went over to her husband. He fretfully muttered words and phrases Sariah could not understand. Her hand burned at the touch of his forehead; his lips were cracked and bleeding. Fear squatted in her heart, an unwelcome guest that neither prayer nor hope could persuade to leave.

"Joshua, Joshua," she said, stroking his cheeks. "Joshua, it is Sariah. I love you more than my own life. Hannah is better. You have to get well too."

She stripped him to the waist and sat for hours bathing him with cool water as he shrank from her touch. She rubbed ointment on his dry lips and fed him tiny spoonfuls of water. When he finally pushed her hand away, she put the bowl down and sat back, covering her face with her hands and praying that when she looked again, the Joshua she loved would be back.

Desperation and exhaustion fought for control of Sariah as she spent the night at Joshua's side, nodding off when exhaustion claimed her, but jerking awake when he cried out or coughed.

Finally, about dawn, while Hannah still slept, Sariah fell into a deep sleep with her hand on Joshua's chest.

While she slept, she dreamed. She and Joshua were young again, dancing in the square of the village, hands clasped as they twirled around, heads tossed back in laughter. Sariah wore Hannah's beautiful dress that swirled behind her.

Around and around they danced, sunlight and music twisting around and through them. The air sparkled with life.

Then slower and slower they danced until they stood facing each other, smiling. Together they looked down between them, and there stood a tiny girl with long dark hair and big eyes. She was Hannah, whole and well. As they reached their arms down in unison to pick the child up, happiness filled Sariah's heart.

But as she cried out at the joy of holding her child, the figures disappeared. A troublesome sound took the place of the music, and Sariah woke with a start to the sound of Joshua's deep coughing.

Pulling herself reluctantly from her imagined happiness, she pushed herself up to see Joshua struggling for breath.

Leaning over him, she could hear wheezing. His eyes were closed, his face gray and his lips blue.

"Joshua, Joshua," she called, an icy fear snaking through her body. She shook him, but when he did not respond, she pulled him up in her arms to sit him up as best she could. "Breathe, Joshua. Hannah is better. She is well. You must get better too."

She nudged his head higher, her words mingling with sobs. "Hannah is well. We will go find the savior. We have the necklace. We will go." On and on, she babbled and begged.

There was no response from him, though; she felt him slipping away from her. Why would he not answer? He always said she was dearer than life to him. He would never give up and leave her.

Between ragged gasps, he went long seconds without breathing.

She began to scream, "I can't do it without you, Joshua." Her pleas turned into a pitiful prayer. "Please, God, don't take Joshua. Please. You healed Hannah. Please heal Joshua. Don't do this to me, God. Please don't do this."

She looked down into Joshua's face to find that his eyes had opened and were fixed on her. His breathing had eased. She gently laid him back on his pillow. Had God answered her prayer?

But a regretful look washed over his face. He reached out his hand, and she grabbed it, kissing it as she had kissed him thousands of times.

He looked into her eyes with love and spoke so quietly she had to bend forward to hear.

"I am so sorry, Sariah. I am so sorry. I love you." He closed his eyes, yet struggled to say something.

Sariah leaned over his lips, her tears dripping onto his face. She caught the quiet words that were his last.

"Tell Hannah I will watch over her in the stars."

He took one more breath, squeezing her hand weakly. She wiped her tears off his face with pleading hands, putting her lips on his and trying to breathe life back into him. His lips turned cold, though, and she pulled away in horror. Rocking back on her knees, she pressed her fists against her face and groaned deeply.

"No, no," she cried, then screamed. "No, no. I can't live without you. Hannah needs you. I need you. God, please, please. Please don't do this to me."

Grabbing his hands, she tried to warm them between hers, but to no avail. After a while, her whole body shaking, she pulled the cover over his face and crawled to the corner at the foot of his bed. She curled up into a ball and covered herself with a blanket, sobbing herself to sleep, her wonderful dream replaced with nightmares that over and over again took her Joshua away from her.

Sariah knew nothing until she felt light on her face and heard a voice calling her. She opened her swollen eyes to see Joanna before her, tears on her cheeks. For one moment of consciousness, Sariah wondered why Joanna was crying, then her world came crashing down around her again as she remembered.

"Oh, Sariah, my poor, poor Sariah," Joanna said, pulling her into her arms. "I am so sorry."

Sariah clung to her until her sobs left every muscle in her body aching. She retched with dry heaves, for her stomach had nothing in it. Behind Joanna, she could see men from the village coming in to wrap Joshua's body for burial.

Joanna held her and rocked her, while her daughters stayed with Hannah and shielded her from the sight of her father being taken out.

Hours later, when she finally stopped crying, Joanna half-carried, half-led Sariah out to the edge of the village where they buried Joshua.

Although Joanna begged, Sariah wouldn't let anyone stay with her the first night. She was too embarrassed by the sheer depth of her agony. If she had not had Hannah to care for, she would have somehow stopped her own breath. As it was, she crawled into her bed, hugged Joshua's cloak to her and prayed she and Hannah would die that night, that the star that had brought Hannah to life would reappear and take them both to Joshua.

It wasn't so, however. Exhausted but afraid to sleep for the nightmares that might come, she sobbed tearlessly.

Her small house with its flickering candles and the lingering smell of sickness seemed a living tomb to her. She covered her face with her hands so she could see nothing that reminded her of Joshua. But there was no part of her that could escape the memory of his touch and love. He was there all around her, and as the darkness of the night deepened, she opened her eyes and strained to imagine him before her, assuring her of his love, promising to return to her.

As she looked up, however, she saw only demons before her. They taunted her from each wall as the firelight made them dance larger, then smaller, then larger again until they reached for her from above. She sat up in her bed with a gasp, her heart in terror's grasp and unable to determine whether she had been awake or asleep.

Stopping only to see that Hannah slept quietly and hoping the demons would follow her out, Sariah turned and ran out the door, letting it shut behind her.

Her feet bare, she half-tripped and half-pulled herself up the stairs to the roof. Crawling to the center, she threw herself prostrate on the floor and clawed at the stones, tearing her nails until they bled.

"Hear my prayer, God," she said, tears once more flowing. "This is too much. I have tried. You know I have tried, but I can't do it any more. It is too much. I can't live without Joshua. He is my strength. I am too weak."

Deep sobs again wracked her body that was already weakened by the trials of the last days. "It's too much; it's too much," she cried over and over. "How can you do this to me when my life is already so hard?"

She didn't know how long she begged God, but when exhaustion stilled her cries, she lay shivering in the chilly night, wishing once more her life would drain both from her and Hannah and release them from whatever trials lay ahead.

Nothing happened, though. Only stillness and darkness surrounded her until her shivering became so intense that, without willing it, she sat up and wrapped her arms around herself.

Slowly, she lifted her eyes to the sky. No clouds marred the deep black. Thousands of stars hung silent and unblinking in their realm. She rose up and knelt underneath their canopy, her heart pleading for their help as one star had helped her so many years ago.

Finally, she asked, simply and tearlessly, "What do you require of me, God? I have nothing else to give."

She bowed her head in submission as the universe held its breath.

Gradually, she felt, rather than saw, the stars begin to twinkle. Warmth began at her head and melted its way through her body, urging her to look up, her arms upstretched to heaven. Within her, a glow spread through her soul as bright as the star the night of Hannah's birth.

Joshua's love and his goodness flowed through her, into every pore and fiber of her being until finally it filled her aching heart and made it throb with the promise that he would always be with her. She hugged herself tightly, trying to make the feeling her prisoner.

Slowly, though, his presence ebbed from her, and she slid again weakly to the ground.

She felt strangely comforted, however. She knew as she lay there for several minutes, maybe hours, that her prayer had been heard. God knew she lived. His eye was on her, even as she had been robbed of the joy of her life. She was somehow sure of that.

With a deep sigh, she finally pulled herself up until she was sitting again and looked above her to the sky that now looked softer. The stars still glimmered, and she smiled up at them, knowing she was smiling up at Joshua.

How she would survive she did not know, but, as she struggled to stand, however much she did not want to live even a minute without Joshua, she knew she would have to and, one day, maybe eventually she could. Her heart still aching, yet filled, she left the rooftop and, holding onto the wall, walked carefully down the stairs.

Her demons had retreated, and the house no longer held terror when she quietly walked through the door. She tiptoed to her own pallet.

Before she could climb into her chilled, empty bed, she heard a small voice.

"Muh, muh," Hannah called. "Muh."

Not knowing what she understood and unable to tell her be still and go back to sleep, Sariah picked up a lantern, turned the wick up, and went over to her.

Hannah lay with big tears on her cheeks.

"Puh? Puh?" she questioned.

Sariah knelt down, placing the lantern on the floor.

"Oh, Hannah, I am so sorry," Sariah told her daughter. "Your father didn't want to leave you, but God wanted him. God took him home, and we have to trust God."

Somehow in her limited understanding of life and death, Hannah seemed to understand that this was a time of great unhappiness. She opened her mouth and wailed.

Sariah pulled the blankets aside and crawled in beside her, wrapping her arms around the tight body of her daughter that shook with inconsolable grief. Drained of her own tears, she kissed Hannah's and begged her to stop, promising her she would take her outside the next day and let her see the sky where her father watched over her. She spoke to her of God's love and how she would never leave her and somehow they would survive without Joshua.

At last, Hannah looked up at Sariah with her eyes wide in the dark and listened to the calm in her mother's voice.

Sariah kissed her swollen eyelids, and just as Hannah slipped into slumber, whispered quietly to her daughter, "We will find the savior. He will make all things right."

As she too fell asleep, that was the thought that brought a small measure of peace to her own broken heart.

15

A Time of Enduring

Somehow Sariah continued to live and breathe and care for Hannah. It was not because she had any desire to live, but only because God, who held the power to take her life, did not choose to do so.

Her hair turned completely gray, and her eyes became weak, her back rounded from lifting Hannah. She still sewed and made beautiful dresses, but her stitches were larger and often crooked. It didn't matter, however, to the women who bought her work. They cared for the woman who faithfully watched over her twisted daughter, often slipping extra coins into their payment, remarking kindly how her sewing only became better through the years.

Hannah remained painfully thin and small, locked in the prison of her tight body. She didn't become ill again, although her fits continued, often tossing her violently against the side of her wagon or the wall where she lay and tearing open her flesh.

Sariah would bandage her and remain inside for days at a time until her wounds healed.

With her arms and legs drawn up, red, festered sores often grew and spread over Hannah's thin skin. Sariah bathed them and spread ointments that people from the village brought from the market. She held her daughter and sang to her or lay beside her to soothe her if touching hurt her too much. Gray began to streak Hannah's long curls as she turned thirty, a day Sariah ignored.

Without speaking of it, the people of the village wrapped their arms around Hannah and Sariah and tried, however impossible the attempt, to take Joshua's place. Men of the village changed their paths in the early morning to stop and lift Hannah into her wagon. Those skilled in carpentry repaired her wagon and crafted a platform for her bed so that Sariah's bent back might have a rest.

Women brought treats to tempt Hannah to eat. They spoke of better days to Sariah and listened with patient, if not understanding, ears as she spoke of her search for the savior and the better life he would bring.

Even those who had turned their backs before at the sight of Hannah now looked with pity upon the two women. Mariam turned into an elderly woman, still bitter at the circumstances God had brought unto her family. She died alone one night in her bed.

Sariah walked with the other villagers when Mariam was buried and stood at the edge of the small gathering as Joanna watched over Hannah. She had picked a thorny flower on the way, and, when the others had left, she made her way to the grave and placed the flower on it.

"I forgive you," Sariah said quietly. "May eternity rest easily upon you."

She went home to Hannah.

Hannah remained patient and content with her life, her eyes sparkling most when Sariah pulled her close and reminded her of her father and the happiness they had enjoyed in the years past. Sariah coaxed her to eat with promises of stories about the long evening walks when Joshua had pulled her in the wagon.

Joanna remained close to her friend and, as Joanna's daughters became women and mothers themselves, they brought their babies to coo at Hannah while Sariah walked to the market or perhaps to the edge of town to visit Joshua's grave.

The years passed slowly and painfully, which seemed to be Sariah's lot.

"What is my future, Joanna?" Sariah asked late one afternoon as one of Joanna's granddaughters played about Hannah's bed. Sariah put a finger in Hannah's fist and helped her touch the child.

Joanna looked regretfully into Sariah's eyes. She grabbed up the baby and bounced her on her knee to Hannah's delight.

"I don't know, my sister." She repeated her kind answer of all the years before.

With Hannah distracted, Sariah asked what she never mentioned in Hannah's presence.

"What if I die? What will happen to her?" She spoke softly and barely nodded down at Hannah.

"We will take care of her," Joanna said. A frown wrinkled her brow. "But, hush, don't speak of such things."

"It could happen, though. Shouldn't I prepare? Hannah is thirty, and I am forty-eight. That is beginning to be old."

Joanna laughed quietly.

"We've been old for a while," she said. She put the baby down and laid her hand on Sariah's arm. "Please don't trouble yourself about that. Remember that the same God who has watched over you in the past will continue in the future. Have faith."

"You sound like Joshua," Sariah said, putting her hand over Joanna's.

"Then I am in good company," Joanna replied.

"Why was Joshua taken from me?" Sariah asked quietly. "The years have been long since he has been gone, and my life stretches ahead of me with loneliness."

"I can't imagine," Joanna replied with a shake of her head. She reached over to put her arm around her friend's shoulder. "I wish I knew why your life is so hard. But there is a sweetness of sacrifice about you that I and others don't have."

Sariah laid her head against Joanna's shoulder. Throughout the years, they'd had this same conversation so many times that it wasn't necessary for either to offer explanations.

Suddenly, Joanna pushed Sariah up as excitement filled her voice.

"I know. Let's put Hannah in her wagon and put the baby beside her to walk to the market. We need to be outside in fresh air."

With practice borne of many years, Joanna and Sariah lifted Hannah into her wagon and put the baby beside her, as they had done with Joanna's babies years before. While Joanna walked beside the cart to watch the child, Sariah picked up the handles, worn smooth by her calloused hands, and pulled the wagon down the street.

Before she got to the end, however, a strong young son of the village came running to her and gently took the wagon handles from her.

"Let me, Sariah," he said. "Maybe if I show off my strength, some beautiful girl will notice me."

She looked into his dark eyes and smiled. He reminded her of Joshua as a young man when he had wanted her to notice his tanned, muscular arms.

"Why, thank you, Benjamin," she said. She stepped aside and followed beside in the narrow dirt road. "What is happening in the market today?"

"Do you mean to say, 'Has anyone heard of the savior?'" he asked with a gentle laugh.

"My friends know me well," Sariah said, returning the laugh.

"They know well of your faith, which is certainly evident in your persistence," Joanna said.

"Perhaps your faithfulness will one day will be rewarded," Benjamin said. "But for now, no, there is no word."

Sariah smiled again. It was the answer she had expected.

The people in her village knew of her endless search and, even when they thought she was chasing after a miracle whose time for fulfillment had long run out, they patiently answered her continuing questioning whether anyone had heard of the long-promised savior.

They reached the small marketplace, and Benjamin placed Hannah under the canopy of the shop where Joshua had worked years before. A few other shops surrounded the open space where roughly hewn tables were set up to display the breads and wares that villagers sold. Goats, sheep, and a few chickens added to the noise of the human voices, vying for sales or catching up on the gossip of the neighborhood.

"Call me when you are ready to return," Benjamin said. "The wagon is light for me."

"Go, Joanna, and look at what you will," Sariah said as Benjamin went to join a group of his friends. "Hannah and I will stay here in the shade."

"Then it will be your turn," Joanna replied. She picked up the baby and walked away.

Sariah bent over Hannah and pulled her up onto her pillows with long practice that she might see some of the activities before her, speaking softly to Hannah of what she saw.

"Look, there is Martha. We have made a dress for her. You helped, remember? You smoothed the cloth down with your hand so that it would be soft for my stitches. And there is Susanna and her new baby. What a pretty baby, but not as pretty as you were."

As usual, Hannah smiled at the attention.

While she spoke mindlessly to Hannah in the endless conversations Hannah never tired of, Sariah's eyes searched out the small crowd to see if there were new faces. Each new person who came into the village became a possibility for her to find out if there was word of a savior.

She looked at the men in the prime of life who looked about Hannah's age, searching their eyes and smiles to find the goodness she sought. The savior would be smart also because Joshua had said he had spoken when he was twelve as if he had authority of God.

"Look, Hannah, who is that man who is buying bread? Does he look like he came from the north?" she asked.

Hannah struggled to lift her head up from the pillows, her legs and arms crossing in the effort. Sariah lifted her head up so she could see.

"Will you be all right if I speak with him?" she asked.

Hannah grunted, and Sariah leaned down to wipe her mouth one last time.

"I will be right back," she said.

Walking quickly to the table of dried fruits where the stranger lingered, Hannah touched him on the sleeve.

"Please, friend, may I ask you a question?" she asked intently.

"What is it, woman?" he replied. "What are you selling?"

"Nothing," she said. "I am looking for a man from the north, a savior who will save Israel."

He looked puzzled.

"I am from the northern villages, but I know of no savior," he replied, turning his attention back to the fruit.

"He would be thirty years old," she said, speaking quickly from practice. "From Nazareth perhaps. The angels sang of his birth, and a star appeared the night he was born."

The stranger laughed, then jerked his arm away from her insistent touching of his sleeve.

"You are speaking nonsense, old woman," he said. "I don't know of any savior."

Her face fell, and she turned away.

"I'm sorry," she said. Shuffling away, she heard him mutter at her foolishness. The merchant, calling his attention back to the fruit, said, "She is harmless. She asks everyone who comes to the village whether they have seen the savior."

Returning to Hannah, Sariah brushed the flies from around her and smiled down at her daughter, who watched the canopy sway in the light breeze.

"He didn't know either, Hannah," she said, "but don't worry. One day someone will answer that he knows of the savior."

She patted Hannah's hand, turning back to look once more for an unfamiliar face in the crowd.

16

Life Changes

In the many years since Joshua had died, Sariah's days remained endless, one seemingly eternal round of the same tasks, the same words and stories told over and over again to Hannah, the same prayers late at night, begging God for strength until the despair passed and calmness settled in enough that she could sleep. In her dreams, she was with Joshua, and he picked her up and eased her burden and loved her again. When she awoke, she would turn to where he used to lie beside her, but, as her reaching arms met only emptiness, her heart realized the truth of what her life was, again, and she curled into herself until she heard Hannah and was forced to face the day.

But, then, one day, her life changed. It wasn't one of those small changes that at the end of the day didn't matter, like finally finishing a dress she was sewing or finding that the tenderness of Hannah's flesh had healed. It was a change that took her breath away.

When Hannah was halfway into her thirty-first year, Sariah had finished feeding her and was washing out the dish when she heard footsteps running to the door that was open to the breeze. As Sariah turned, Joanna appeared, coughing with exertion. She held to the side of the door to catch her breath.

Sariah rushed to her side.

"Joanna, what's wrong? Are the children all right?" She laid an arm across her friend's back.

"They are fine," Joanna said, trying to take deep breaths. "I've run from the market."

Sariah laughed. "You are too old to run, my friend."

"It is the savior," she said, grabbing Sariah's arms. "I believe your savior lives."

For the briefest of moments, Sariah could not speak. She shook her head in puzzlement.

"The savior? Tell me, what did you hear?" The color drained from her face as Sariah brought both hands to cover her mouth. It was the moment she had lived for, but now she could not believe the words she was hearing.

Her knees became weak. She pulled Joanna by the arms over to the table and pushed her down on the bench, falling to sit beside her.

"Is he here? Tell me," she insisted.

Joanna's eyes were wide as she still struggled for breath.

"A stranger in the marketplace from far away speaks of a great teacher, a man who can perform miracles."

"Miracles? What miracles?" Sariah shook Joanna gently as if to force the words faster from her mouth.

"He said the lame can walk and the blind can see when this man touches them. He speaks of the kingdom of God and what men must do to enter it." She hugged Sariah, laughing. "It must be the savior you have sought for so long. You are right. You have always been right."

Sariah jumped to her feet, clasping Joanna's shoulders once again in excitement. "Is he still here in the village?"

Joanna nodded. "I told him he had to stay until I brought someone who had been waiting for him."

"Will you stay with Hannah while I go?"

"Of course," she said, urging Sariah in the direction of the door. "He is a tall, dark man with a long beard. He is waiting for you."

Sariah ran as best she could down the narrow road, stopping several times to hold onto the sides of buildings to regain her breath. Once she fell and tore open the palm of her hand but pulled herself up again, holding it, bleeding, against her.

Reaching the market, she looked wildly from one side to the other to find the man Joanna had described. When she did not see him, she ran from person to person, begging them to help her find him. But no one seemed to know what she was talking about. Several she didn't know pushed her aside.

She saw her friend Martha at the edge of the crowd, speaking to another woman. Half stumbling, Sariah made her way to her. Her energy spent, she pulled at Martha's sleeve, but sobs took away her words.

"Sariah, what's wrong?" she asked. "You're bleeding." She took Sariah's cut hand in hers.

"It's nothing," Sariah answered, pulling her hand away from Martha. "Where is the man who knows of the savior?"

Martha clucked her tongue in gentle chiding. "Sariah, you must stop worrying people about a savior."

"A tall man with a dark beard, Joanna said. Where is he?" Sariah turned to search again and started to walk away, but Martha pulled her back.

"I have seen that man," she said. "He is there in the carpenter shop with Josiah." She motioned to the small shop across the street.

Without stopping to answer, Sariah began running again,

pushing people aside as she struggled to get to the shop.

Breathless once more when she reached the wide door that opened onto the square, she stumbled inside and called loudly for Josiah, the carpenter.

He stepped from the darkness at the back of the shop with the tall bearded man.

"Why, Sariah, what is it? Is Hannah all right?" he asked, walking toward her. "Your hand is bleeding."

Brushing his questions aside, she knelt at the feet of the stranger and grabbed his hem with her bloodied hands.

"Please, you spoke of a savior who can work miracles. Where is he? I must know where he is." She reached up for his hands.

The man seemed taken aback but helped Josiah as he pulled Sariah up and led her to a stool where they sat her gently down. Josiah reached for a clean rag to tie up her hand.

"My name is Joel," the stranger said gently. "Who are you?"

"Sariah," she answered, still gasping to catch her breath, "and I have searched for the savior for so many years. Do you know about him? Do you know where he is?"

"I don't know if he is the savior, but I do know of a godly man who seems to work miracles wherever he walks. His name is Jesus."

"Jesus?" she asked. She searched his face for understanding, beginning to calm down at his soft voice.

"Those who have never walked stand up and walk, those who have never seen can see, and those who cannot hear can hear." He stretched his arms reverently toward the ceiling. "He speaks of God as his father, and multitudes follow him."

"He heals people?" Her head was light with imaginings. "I have searched for the savior since his star brought Hannah to life, but I've . . . I've never really known why. I hoped he could make Hannah better, but . . . it seemed more like a dream."

She bowed her head as tears fell, and she trembled when faced with the knowledge she had awaited for so long, not even realizing what that knowledge would be. Hannah healed? She could not speak at the possibility. In all her thoughts of the savior through the many years and her believing that he would somehow make their lives better, she had hoped he could make Hannah well, but had she really ever believed he could? Make Hannah walk and talk? If he did it to others, why not her Hannah?

Puzzled, Joel asked, "Hannah?" But still she could not speak.

"Her daughter," Josiah explained. He brought Sariah a cup of water and held it to her lips. "She is stricken with the palsy. She has never walked or talked."

Swallowing the water, Sariah looked up, hope shining through the tears filling her eyes.

"I must take her to see the savior. Where is this Jesus? Please tell me where I can find him." The panic crept back into her voice, which trembled as she reached for Joel's hands again.

Joel gently placed her hands in one of his strong ones and patted them with the other.

"He travels," he said. "Multitudes follow him out up into the mountainsides where he teaches them. Others bring their children, their brothers and sisters, their friends on pallets to lay before him for healing." His eyes got a faraway look. "I saw him only once—in Galilee where he healed a leper, who shed his rags and ran away on strong limbs."

"But where he is now?" Sariah insisted. "Why won't you tell me?"

He looked down with compassion upon her. "I don't know where he is now. That was many months ago. His travels are mostly in the north. Perhaps he stays there because I have heard he makes the leaders of the faith of Israel angry."

"Who would be angry at such a man?" Josiah asked.

"He says he is the son of God, and for many in authority that is blasphemy." Joel shrugged his shoulders. "It doesn't seem to matter to those whom he heals."

"And it doesn't matter to me," Sariah said. "I must find him. Can you take me to him?"

"Oh, my daughter," he said, patting her hands again. "I don't know where he is. He was in the north around Galilee when I saw him, and that was months ago."

She bowed her head and took a deep breath.

Then with the resolve born of many years of clinging to hope when there was none apparent, she looked up and said, "I will find him. I will go north."

Joel looked at Josiah, his eyes appealing for help.

"Sariah, Hannah cannot travel," Josiah said with sorrow in his voice. "She is too frail. She doesn't have the strength to make a trip, and you don't either."

She hesitated only a moment, then spoke empathically.

"Then I will go and bring him here to her. I have that beautiful necklace Ishmael gave me. I will give it to him if he will come."

Joel shook his head. "I think this man cares nothing for jewels. I have heard he tells people not to seek for the riches of the world, but for those of heaven."

"Then tell me what I must do," she insisted. She looked from one man to another, pleading with her eyes.

When the men only looked at each other, saying nothing, she asked, "What would you do if Hannah were your child?"

A thick quietness hung in the air, then they both looked at Sariah.

"I will be back in six months for the marriage of my brother in a nearby town," Josiah finally said. "Before that time, my journeys will take me north this spring. I will inquire about this Jesus and return with word."

"I will give you my necklace," she said. "It is very beautiful."

He shook his head gently. "I don't want your necklace. I haven't even known you before this day, yet I have not seen so much faith since my mother took her last breath. She told me to find the path in life that God intended for me and to walk it. Perhaps this is on that path."

"But I can't wait," she said, wringing her hands, then wincing at the pain. "I have waited for so long."

"If it is good, it will happen," Josiah said gently. "This is more than you have ever had to hope for. You can put the time to good use. You can spend your time strengthening Hannah and yourself if you must make a journey."

"I promise I will return," Joel said sincerely. "I want to see this man again also. Perhaps he is the savior all of Israel has waited for, and I needed the faith of a humble mother in a tiny village to help me see it."

Sariah sighed. It was indeed more than she had ever had. She had lived too long with the hope in her heart to give up when at last she had a real hope to cling to. She would wait. She had to.

17

A Long Wait

So Sariah again waited. Through the long winter and into the spring. As the months of the year crept on, the same as the last, more and more news of the man with the healing touch came to the village. Each new story made Sariah's heart first leap with joy and then drop to discouragement as she wondered when Hannah's turn would come. The prayer on her lips in the morning was that the day might bring the savior to Hannah. Every night her last whispered words were, "Tomorrow. Please let it be tomorrow."

The stories she told Hannah now throughout their long days together were not so much of the happiness in the days past when Joshua shared their lives but of anticipation of the future when the man called Jesus would take her into his arms and she would walk. Sariah tried to imagine and could not, but she shook her head against her inability, then urged her heart to cling stubbornly to the thought that one day it just might be.

"Do you think it could happen? Could Hannah really walk one day?" Sariah asked Joanna as they sat at the table sewing a hem in a dress while Hannah napped.

"Oh, Sariah, you have asked me so many times," Joanna teased. "Do you think my answer has changed?"

"But, again, tell me. How could it be?" She folded the material around her arms and looked away, trying to conjure such a miracle. "My mind can't even imagine seeing Hannah walk and talk."

"If the joy in such a sight would match the long time you have waited, then your joy will be almost too much to bear," Joanna answered.

"But when? When can I take her to him?" Sariah asked as she had before.

"Wait until the man Joel comes back, and then we will see," Joanna answered as she had also done many times before.

Sariah sighed. "You're right. It can't be much longer."

Joanna pushed a plate of bread in front of her. "He told you to eat and get strong."

"I will try." Picking up a piece of bread, she brought it to her lips and took a bite, not even tasting it as she once again contemplated what the future might be.

While she waited, Sariah prepared, sewing a soft lining for a small box where she carefully laid the necklace she would present to the savior. Next she sewed a dress made of delicate material for Hannah to wear when she would see this Jesus. Under the bodice, she sewed several layers of thicker cloth so when Hannah drooled, her dress would not be wet. With her dress on and her beautiful hair brushed out until it shone, Jesus would not be able to pass her daughter by.

For herself, she sewed a humble dress of sturdy cloth able to withstand what might be a long journey.

Remembering what she and Joshua had planned years before, she calculated how much it would cost to buy a small wagon that could be drawn by a donkey if she needed to take Hannah outside the village, perhaps to Jerusalem, to meet the savior. The thought of leaving her village filled her with fear that forced her to her knees to ask God that he somehow send Jesus to her so she would not have to go to him. She had not left the village since Hannah had been born years before. But arising from her prayers, she knew either that God would not require her to leave or that she would somehow find the strength.

Joanna disagreed with her plan to buy a wagon.

"You can't travel that far, Sariah," she said. "We are old women now, and there are dangers in the road."

"Then I will pay a strong young man to take me," Sariah answered stubbornly. She looked at Joanna and could see the pity in her eyes, but they couldn't be upset at each other for long.

Then, realizing the chances of Sariah actually beginning such a journey, she said, "If you must go, we will go with you."

Sariah agreed, knowing she would never ask that of her, and then did not speak of it further to Joanna.

But Joanna later shook her head as Sariah put coins in the hands of the village carpenter and asked him to build a small wagon that Hannah could lie in and a donkey could pull. It took Sariah weeks to get up enough nerve to purchase the donkey, but finally she did so and asked the carpenter if the small animal could graze alongside his own in a pen behind his shop. She paid him a coin every week for hay and water for the donkey. When finished, the wagon stood beside her home in a narrow alley.

Throughout the months, as time seemed to slow its course even more, Sariah forced herself to eat so that she would not appear weak and wan before the savior. Between every meal and before she put Hannah to bed, she patiently fed her as much as she could entice her to eat, until, finally, Hannah would turn her head and refuse to open her mouth again.

Hannah, who had turned thirty-three, listened to Sariah's endless stories about the savior and how he had helped people just like Hannah to walk and run and talk. The tales of the savior became intertwined with Sariah's hope until Hannah became a beautiful princess with many under her command to do this and that at her bidding. Hannah loved the stories, twisting and turning on her bed with delight and squealing until she choked on her spit and Sariah had to roll her over and pound on her back.

Even more and more tales of the man who commanded miracles came to the village—tales so fantastic many denied them or struggled to believe.

But Sariah did believe.

Each story brought joy to her—and with it desperation that she would not be able to see him, not be able to take Hannah to him, not be able to convince the savior to heal her daughter. People listened to her cares, but Sariah heard them whisper words of pity behind her back. She knew they didn't believe that Hannah could be made whole. With sadness, she became quiet, pouring out her heart only to God and less often to Joanna, now distracted with the care of a daughter who was carrying a child with difficulty and suffered constant illness.

The day finally came, however, when spring arrived and green dotted the landscape beyond the houses. The bleating of new lambs wafted down from the hills on a warm breeze.

And Sariah began to stand at the door for hours daily to watch for Joel.

18

A Friend Returns

One afternoon, Sariah heard a knock on the door. It was Joel. She opened the door to the welcome sight.

"You are here!" she cried.

Pulling him inside, she kissed his hands.

"I promised I would come," he said with a laugh. "Come, let us sit down."

They sat at the table, Sariah hardly able to speak with excitement.

"What of the savior? Does he indeed live? Where is he?" she insisted.

"He does, and his miracles grow," Joel said, his hands outstretched. "There are tales of lepers restored to wholeness, demons cast out, and even one man brought back to life after being dead for several days."

"Did you see him?" she asked.

"I did, although it is hard," Joel said. "Multitudes press around him wherever he goes. But he is followed by a band of faithful followers who travel with him. I spoke to one of them one night."

Sariah gasped. "You did? What did he say?" Her eyes remained fixed on his face in anticipation.

"I asked him who this Jesus was."

"What did he say?" She leaned forward in her stool, her hands in her lap. Joel put his hand over hers. "Tell me—what did he say?"

"He said Jesus is the son of God," Joel whispered.

"Do you think he is?" Sariah asked fervently. "I do."

Joel hesitated but a second. "I do also."

"Where is he? Oh please, tell me he is close," she pleaded.

"He is close," Joel said softly. "He travels throughout the country around Jerusalem now, and there are many who are angered with him. They say he is blasphemous. I am afraid some have it in their hearts to hurt him."

Tears filled Sariah's eyes. "Please, no," she begged him. "Please, I must go to him. I must take Hannah."

He looked at her with sympathy. "You cannot make a journey," he said. "Look at your thin arms." He glanced over at where Hannah lay on the bed. "Your daughter seems so frail."

"I am strong, though," she said. "I have lifted Hannah since she was little. I can still carry water from the well."

He contemplated her attempts to show him how strong her arms were and smiled gently.

"Oh, Sariah, what faith you have." He sighed. "When I return from my brother's wedding, we will talk. I will help you get to the savior."

He opened his arms, and they embraced, his shoulder wet when he finally let her go and said good-bye.

She did not see Joanna until the next day, but when she did, her first words were "We must go find the savior now. I feel it is time." She looked at Joanna expectantly as she told her of Joel's visit.

They stood outside Sariah's door. Joanna had stopped on her way to visit her daughter, whose baby would arrive any day.

"But we can't go with you now," Joanna answered. She looked at Sariah with sad eyes. "Even now, Rachel has the pains of childbirth. She is sick, and I must stay with her."

Sariah smiled regretfully. "I know."

"Wait until your friend returns and Rachel has regained her strength. Then we'll go with you," she said.

Grabbing Sariah's hands, Joanna pleaded with her eyes and touch for Sariah to listen to her.

Sariah bowed her head for a moment and then looked up at her friend, smiling regretfully.

"You're right," she said quietly. "We'll wait. I'm good at that."

But throughout the day she could not rid herself of the feeling that this was the time for which she and Hannah, and Joshua as he watched over them, had waited. She did her tasks more routinely than ever, telling Hannah the words she had spoken so many times before, but with an excitement, a conviction growing within her that occupied her every thought.

When night came, she slept fitfully, waking up often to listen to a voice within her that seemed to speak that it was time, that this was the time for which Hannah had been born.

She finally fell into a deep sleep right before dawn and woke after the sun rose when Hannah began calling her name.

As she got up, her mind was immediately clear and her path straight before her. She and Hannah would go and find the savior. She wouldn't tell anyone for they would beg her not to make the trip. She wouldn't ask anyone to go with her, for she and Hannah would either find the savior or they would die together.

Throughout the day, she prepared. She slowly pulled Hannah in the wagon to the marketplace where she bought extra dried fruit and fish and bread. When someone remarked how hungry she must be to buy so much food, she smiled and said, "Hannah needs to eat more so that she will be bigger." No one could argue with that.

Putting a coin into the hand of a young man, she asked him to carry two jugs of water back to her house where she carefully filled all the smaller jugs she had and hid them with the food under blankets. She pulled the smaller wagon into the house and left it waiting close to Hannah's bed.

Carefully bathing Hannah and washing her hair, she combed it out and braided it tightly. She leaned over and kissed Hannah, whispering in her ear that they were at last going to see the savior and that she must be brave and strong. Hannah's eyes grew big and wondering.

She urged Hannah to eat throughout the day to store strength against their journey. Hannah patiently opened her mouth and took the cereal and bread soaked in broth. Afterwards, Sariah wrapped up a bowl of cereal and added it to the food she had collected.

When the day was finally over, Sariah put Hannah to bed and, after she had fallen asleep, lit a lamp, and removed the box with the necklace and the bag with her money, tucking them into the wagon.

After checking to see that Hannah still slept, she walked slowly, with deliberateness and reverence, up to the temple of her roof to petition God one last time.

The sky that she knelt under was warm and clear. The stars blinked compassionately upon their friend. Ignoring her stiff knees and the pain in her back from her busy day, she bowed her head and closed her eyes.

"It is Sariah, dear God, coming once more to thank thee for thy care and keeping," she said softly.

Her long, gray hair fell down from her head and onto the hands that through the years had become knotted and veined. Two silent tears overflowed the banks of the lines and wrinkles on her face.

"I'm going to take thy blessed child, Hannah, to find the savior. Watch over us and guide us there safely, I pray."

There was nothing else to say. She ended with an almost inaudible "amen."

No thundering voice answered, nor even a still, small voice that pierced her soul. There was, however, as she looked up, or so it seemed, one star in the north that shined more brightly than the others. She smiled up at it.

"Thank you, Joshua," she said.

Resolved, she pushed herself to her feet and climbed down the stairs to sleep for a few hours until their journey began.

19

A Journey Begins

Sariah knew she would awake when it was time, and she did. There were still about two hours before sunrise when she suddenly awoke refreshed. Quickly putting on the dress she had laid out, she said a prayer over Hannah that she would be safe until she returned from her errand.

The moonlight showed her the way to the donkey's pen, where she quietly tied a rope around its neck and led it back to the house. Not used to handling animals, it took her awhile to place the donkey in its small yoke at the wagon and lead it to the front of her home. Afraid that others might hear, she worked quietly, but at the end, with the wagon and donkey finally in front of the door, her heart was beating fast and beads of sweat dotted her forehead.

Inside, she awoke Hannah, telling her not to be afraid, but that they were going to go on a trip. Hannah blinked against the light and kept dozing back to sleep as her mother cleaned her and dressed her in her new dress.

"You are beautiful," she told Hannah, kissing her as she smiled sleepily.

Then the moment came that Sariah had feared. Would she be able to lift Hannah into the larger wagon? Through the years, she had not even thought about how heavy Hannah was—she had just lifted her. But could she lift her up and into the higher wagon? She prayed strength would be hers.

"Hannah, be light," she said, bending over and putting her arms under her shoulders and knees. She easily lifted her into the smaller wagon as she had so many times before and pulled it outside the door. The donkey startled at the sight, but she patted and hushed him until he rested quietly again.

Then, with one mighty heave, she lifted Hannah up and over the side of the wagon onto the bedding.

"Angels helped me, Hannah," she said, smiling down at her. Hannah's eyes were wide with fright, and she began shaking with the newness of the wagon and the nearness of the donkey. Fearing one of her fits would take hold, Sariah stroked her and talked to her in whispers until her eyes were full of trust again. When she was stilled, Sariah covered her with blankets, pulled the smaller wagon back into the house, closed the door, and took her place at the donkey's head.

The morning was still deep in darkness as they walked through the village. With the wagon rattling behind her, Sariah worried that people might hear her and stop them, but although two lamps came on in the houses behind them, no one came to the doors and called to the little group heading down the road.

Sariah walked resolutely beside the donkey, leading it slowly so as not to bounce Hannah too much over the rough spots in the road. Hannah dozed with the motion of the cart, jerking awake when the wagon hit a rut. They left the village behind them and walked in the dark with the moon and the stars overhead.

An hour later, they were still alone as the sun began to peek over the horizon to the right. Hills dotted with the greenness of spring dwarfed them, their height menacing to Sariah as she struggled to look ahead to the road and keep panic from rising within her. She breathed deeply and thought of the moment they would see the savior.

As an hour, then two, passed under the rising sun, she became more used to the hills and tried to ignore the pain in her back and the soreness of her feet that were unaccustomed to walking for such a long distance. Blisters were already beginning to burn on her feet.

As slowly as she was walking, she thought Jerusalem must be at least three hours away. When she reached there, she would offer a coin to someone to let her rest under their shade. Surely, no one could refuse to help a woman such as she with a daughter as special as Hannah.

She wished she could marvel at the countryside as one who had not been without the reaches of her village for so many years, but instead she fought the fear in her heart as she saw unfamiliar land. She had heard tales of thieves on the road, who robbed and beat people and left them for dead.

To stifle the terror that would turn her back, she spoke to God and to Joshua, telling them of her journey and begging for their presence. With the sun now climbing the sky, she missed the stars that usually listened to her prayers. The sun, although it began to warm her, did not comfort her but added its own threats of thirst and heat.

No people traveled the road yet, although Sariah saw two shepherds with a flock on a nearby hill stop and watch her for a while. She felt no danger from them, though, and turned her head away.

She kept moving, slowly, one labored step after another, until she heard Hannah whimpering.

"It is all right, Hannah," she said. "We will take a break from our journey."

She led the donkey over to a group of small trees that offered some shade and tied him to a small branch, then hobbled back to the side of the wagon. Hannah blinked against the sunlight, her face contorted and her cheeks beginning to burn from the sun.

Taking a light shawl from around Hannah's shoulders, she gently laid it across her forehead to shield her eyes.

"Are you hungry?" she asked. "I am hungry, so I know you must be."

With difficulty, Sariah pulled herself up onto the wagon and over the crude bench that stretched across the front. There wasn't much room in the bed of the wagon where Hannah lay, but Sariah crawled on hands and knees to reach behind her and pull out the water and food she had brought.

Hannah smiled, which comforted Sariah.

She knelt and poured water that still remained cool from the night into a cup and, awkwardly pulling Hannah's head up into her arms, gave her sips of water and then noisily finished it off herself.

Laying Hannah back down, she said, "Now, Hannah, you must eat for me so you will have strength for the day. Your cereal will not be warm as it usually is, but you must eat it, and you must be careful not to choke."

Hannah nodded, and Sariah said, "Good girl."

Still kneeling, she stirred a little water into Hannah's cereal and began spooning it into her mouth. For herself, she hungrily stuffed her mouth full of bread, following it with water to moisten it.

When Hannah had finished what cereal had not dripped from her mouth, Sariah gave her more water and then dipped some bread into the water for her to suck on. To Sariah's relief, she ate well.

"Do you hurt?" she asked her. Hannah shook her head.

"Good. I will go slowly so the wagon will not jar you," she said, "but you must be brave and quiet. Think thoughts of the savior. He is ahead of us, and we will find him. Think of your father who loved us so much. He is with us. Even if we cannot see his star during the day, it is there."

She laid Hannah back, cushioning her with the blankets and pillows, and draped the shawl loosely over her eyes to shield them.

"Do not be afraid," she reassured Hannah, wishing someone were there to tell her the same thing.

By the time she crawled back and climbed down painfully onto the hard ground again, her strength had left her, and she held on to the side of the wagon, leaning over and trying to breathe slowly once more. With her head bent, she saw blood on her feet and knew that she must bandage them. She had not thought to bring bandages, so she chewed at the hem of her dress until she made a small hole and could tear the bottom off into two long strips. Those she wrapped around her feet as best she could, ignoring the rawness of the open blisters. Standing up straight again, she cried out at the soreness in her back.

The donkey was eating the leaves off the shrubs, oblivious to the trials around him. Untying the rope and pulling him away from the green, tender leaves, she limped back onto the road and continued.

As the morning drew on, Sariah saw a group of perhaps six travelers walking ahead on the road. Her hands began shaking, and she struggled to breathe for the fear that gripped her and slowed her steps.

Knowing that it was not customary for a woman to travel alone, she pulled the donkey and wagon off the road. At the side of the wagon, she loosely covered Hannah with the shawl and begged her to not make a sound. With a frantically beating heart, she returned to the donkey and busied herself with looking over him, as if she feared he had hurt himself.

As the group approached, they called out and, struggling to find voice, she called back.

"Is anything wrong?" one of the men asked. They stopped.

"I was just making sure my donkey had not hurt his leg," she answered. "But he did not."

"Are you alone?" another said kindly.

"My . . . my husband is ahead," she said. "I go to meet him."

"We saw no one," the man said.

"He is in the hills," she said.

They looked at each other in puzzlement.

"Are you sure you need no help?" the first man asked.

"I am sure," she said. "Please, continue your journey. But how far is Jerusalem? We have family there." She forced herself to speak slowly and with calmness.

"A one-hour walk for the young and strong," one said. "But with your wagon, perhaps it is two or three."

"Thank you," she said. With trembling hands, she turned back to the donkey, fumbling with his harness. She could hear the men talking among themselves, but they soon walked on.

Relief weakened her, and she stumbled to the side of the wagon and sank to the ground, willing herself to stop shaking.

She sat with her hands covering her face and prayed for strength until she heard Hannah whimper "Muh, Muh."

With difficulty, she pulled herself up by the side of the wagon and, pulling the shawl away, looked in on Hannah. Tears filled Hannah's eyes, and her lips were dry.

"It is fine," Sariah said. "I am fine. The nice men just wanted to know if we needed help. They are on their way, and we will be soon. Do you hurt?"

Hannah nodded, and Sariah touched her until Hannah whimpered when her hand reached behind to her back.

"Is it your back against the wagon?" she asked. Hannah jerked and cried out as her mother rubbed her back.

Tears now came to Sariah's eyes.

"Oh, I am so sorry. You are not used to such a rough journey."

Tenderly, she cushioned Hannah as best she could with what she had and told her how wonderful it would be when she could walk and not have to lie on her back in the wagon. She tipped Hannah's head up and poured tiny swallows of water down her throat, then wet her fingers and rubbed the moisture on Hannah's lips. She drank thirstily herself, for now the sun was high in the sky and burning down on them. Carefully, she placed the water back in the wagon, saying a silent prayer that it would last them for their journey.

"Come," she said to the donkey again and trudged back to the road. She met others on the road, but each time when she saw them in the distance, she would pull off the road and hide behind the donkey until they passed. No other travelers spoke to her, hardly paying any attention to the woman with the hair that now straggled down around her sun-reddened face and with bloodied bandages around her feet.

For another hour, they traveled thus, slower and slower, stopping every few minutes to rewrap her feet and comfort Hannah, who was now hot and whimpering.

"We are almost there," she promised Hannah, hoping in her heart it was true. "Please, be brave."

Hannah finally slept, and Sariah, one labored step at a time, climbed a little hill. Surely Jerusalem could not be much farther. There, she could rest under someone's shady awning or a tree. She would take out some of her coins from their hiding place and offer them in exchange for a place to rest and cool water from a well. Surely no one could deny her that.

That thought kept her going for just a few more steps . . . and then a few more.

20

A Meeting with Evil

The trip up the next hill exhausted her, but she looked ahead to the bottom and then the crest of another just a short way off with a small bush or two. When she had reached that, she would stop and feed Hannah and her own grumbling stomach. Perhaps at the top of that hill she would see the end of her journey. She did not even look down at her throbbing feet. To do so might discourage her.

She jerked at the donkey, who suddenly did not want to move.

"Come," she said. "We must go."

So busy was she with him that she did not see the five men who came over the other hill and stopped, pointing to them.

Urging the donkey on with promises of hay she did not have, she finally convinced him to move, and they started down the hill.

Suddenly, she heard the sound of loud laughter and looked

away from the donkey to see the men coming toward them. She stopped, yanking on the donkey's rope now to stop him, looking for a place to hide, but there was none. She was afraid to get off the path on the decline, but there seemed to be no other choice. Her heart was pounding so hard she could feel it in her throat.

Praying with all her heart that the movement would not hurt Hannah, she carefully led the donkey off the road. It was not smooth terrain, however, and she heard Hannah cry out.

She stopped, torn between Hannah's pain and her own fear. The men were close enough for her to see that they were dressed in filthy clothes and had long, dirty beards with rags tied around their heads. Their hands and feet were black and grimy, and they spoke and laughed crudely. One of them called out to her to stop as they came closer.

As quickly as she could on her tender feet, she hid behind the side of the wagon, reaching to pull the shawl down over Hannah again.

"Do not make a noise, Hannah," she whispered. Leaning down, she pretended to look at the wheel, hoping they would consider her too poor and humble to bother.

They came closer, however, and stood at the donkey. She looked up, trying to appear brave, but she knew she failed. Suddenly, she could hardly breathe.

"Old woman, what are you doing?" one of them said roughly. His dark eyes glittered meanly, and he opened his mouth in a wicked smile that showed rotting teeth.

"I am meeting my husband," she said, her voice shaking. She clung to the side of the wagon, knowing if she let go, she would fall to the ground. These must be some of the robbers of which people had spoken. Their unwashed odor gagged her.

"I see no husband," he said. Turning to the other men, he asked with a laugh. "Do you see a husband?"

They all laughed, and all but the one who stayed by the donkey moved around to the opposite side of the wagon.

One of them stepped up and looked into the wagon where Hannah was covered.

"And who is this?" he asked, grinning. He pulled the shawl back, but Sariah reached across the wagon bed and, strengthened by fright, pulled the shawl from him.

"It is my daughter. Leave her alone. You have no need of her," she said, aware that her voice was quavering.

"Your daughter? Let us see."

He roared in laughter at her frail attempts to protect Hannah and threw the shawl to the ground. Hannah's eyes widened and a guttural scream of terror broke forth from her mouth as he leaned into her.

"What is wrong with her?" he demanded.

"She is palsied," Sariah pleaded. "Please, leave us alone. We have done nothing to you." Sobs that could no longer be denied broke from her chest. She resisted the urge to fall to her hands and knees and crawl under the wagon for what little protection that would offer, knowing that to do so would leave Hannah defenseless. As best as she could, she shielded Hannah with her own thin arms.

Glancing around wildly, she saw the robber at the end of the wagon unhook the donkey but could see no one else on the road that might help her. She and Hannah were alone in the barren landscape with embodied evil as their unsought companions.

"No, don't take my donkey," she cried. "We must go find the savior. The savior . . . he will make my daughter well." Her distressed babbling only humored the men further.

"See if there is any food in the wagon," the robber said. "We want nothing of these wretched women. They have nothing for men such as us. "

Roaring raucously, the men began to plow through the wagon, being careful not to touch Hannah in seeming disgust of her condition.

They quickly discovered the water and bread and passed the jugs around, draining them sloppily into their mouths. The other food they divided up among themselves with villainous glee. Finished with the water, they threw the small jugs onto the ground where they shattered.

"We will perish out here," Sariah begged them. "Please have mercy on my daughter and me."

"There is no mercy in this world," one of them replied.

"What is this?" another man asked suddenly, pulling out the necklace box and the bag of coins. He tossed the bag to one of the men, who emptied the money into his hand, grunting in delight. The other opened the box and thrust it forward so that all might see the necklace glitter in the sunlight.

Sariah stood helpless as Hannah whimpered. For once, she had no comfort to give her child, for her own terror paralyzed her.

"Where did such a pitiful one as you get such a jewel?" he demanded.

"It is my gift for the savior," she answered between sobs. "Please don't take it. I must give it to the savior so that he will heal my daughter."

"You speak nonsense, woman." Dropping the necklace down into his dirty cloak, he looked around and then down at Hannah, who was now wailing. "Make her be quiet."

Sariah patted her and begged her to stop crying, but to no avail.

"Silence," he demanded again. One of the men next to him pulled a knife from his sash and stepped forward, looking to his leader for guidance.

Sariah screamed and tried vainly to climb into the wagon to put herself between Hannah and the knife. They laughed at her feeble efforts.

Hannah wailed louder. The leader hesitated as the man with the knife awaited his word.

At that moment, with a horrible noise, Hannah began shaking in a fit. Her eyes rolled back in their sockets, and her arms and legs shook more intensely than Sariah had ever seen, so violently that her body was lifted off the bed of the wagon. She thrashed wildly, foaming at the mouth, gritting her teeth.

Sariah stood helpless as time slowed, then stopped.

The men jumped back and stared. The man with the knife lowered his arm and with eyes opened in fright yelled, "She has a demon."

They stepped back even farther.

"I have seen it before," he said. "She is possessed of a demon." Shoving the knife back into his sash, he turned and ran, slipping in the rocky soil. Others followed at his insistence. The man by the donkey scrambled up to the road, dropping the rope in his haste. The donkey ran off.

The leader, however, seemed transfixed by the sight of Hannah, whose misery continued. And Sariah stood shaking, unable to take her eyes off of his face, knowing that his decision meant their lives or a sad death in the desert.

Finally, in what seemed an eternity, the leader turned and spat on the ground.

"Death would be too merciful for you," he said. He turned to follow his men, who stood at the top of the hill, urging him to come.

Sariah clung to the side of the wagon, terrified they would return and hurt them. Unable to move, unable to speak until she saw that they had disappeared over the hill, she could only watch helplessly as Hannah's fit ran its course and left her limp and unconscious in the wagon, her face turned away from her mother.

Knowing she could never forgive herself for abandoning Hannah in her need, Sariah fought the desire to fall to the ground and relieve her weak legs of their burden. She watched the hill until she heard their voices get farther and farther away, then turned to Hannah.

"Hannah, Hannah," she said, shaking her shoulder. "Hannah, they are gone. Hannah, please, look at me." Her voice trembled, but became stronger as her mind turned to her daughter. She took her by the chin and turned her face toward her.

Hannah's dark eyes opened and fixed on Sariah, their darkness turned black against the paleness of her skin. With shaking hands, Sariah wiped the spittle off of her mouth. Her lip was torn and bleeding at the corner. She lay gasping.

Sariah pulled herself along the wagon to the other side where the broken pottery lay on the ground. Dropping to her knees, she clawed at the pieces until she found one with a tiny puddle of water in it. Cradling the pottery piece in her hands, she walked as fast as she could without spilling the precious load.

She picked up Hannah's head and slowly poured the water into her mouth. Hannah sputtered at the drink, then turned her head back and closed her eyes.

Unable to deny her weakness any longer, Sariah sank to her knees on the rocky soil and banged her fists against the ground until they too were torn and bleeding, deep sobs welling forth from her years of suffering.

Long minutes later, when her despair ran its course to exhaustion, she sat back and looked to heaven, closing her eyes against the sharp sunlight.

"It is all I have, God," she cried, her hands palm up against her thighs. "I can't do it any more. There is nothing left. I cannot pull the wagon myself."

She repeated the same words, over and over, until at last, there was nothing else she could say.

But no voice answered her. The only sound was the screech of a bird high in the sky. There was no comfort in that.

Finally, there were no tears left, no words left to pray. With deliberateness, she pulled herself to her feet and, ignoring her bloodied hands and feet, climbed into the wagon and crawled over to where Hannah now lay asleep, color slowly returning to her face.

She gently wiped the blood from Hannah's mouth and, lying down, put one arm under Hannah's head to cushion it, then pulled the shawl over their faces to protect them from the sun. Her other arm she put across Hannah and drew her close as she had done so many times before. She kissed her on her soft cheek and laid her own head down.

The last words she uttered before she closed her own eyes and prepared to die were, "I'm sorry, Joshua. I tried."

To God, she said, "Please, let Hannah die before me."

2 1

Journey's End

Sariah did not know how long she slept under the hot sun, but she awoke when voices pushed into the edge of her consciousness. A moment of wondering, and then she was filled with unspeakable fear again. She tightened her hold on Hannah and prayed to God, who had denied her the death she sought, to protect them.

Trembling, she held her breath as the footsteps approached on the road, nearer and nearer. She unwillingly whimpered deep in her throat.

Then she heard voices of kindness, coming closer. Even those disappointed her, though, because she would rather have died.

The footsteps, which sounded like many, came to the wagon and stopped. Sariah held her breath again and closed her eyes tightly.

"See who hides there, John," she heard a strong, smooth voice say.

The voice reminded her of Joshua many years before when he would hold her close and whisper words of love and comfort to her late at night. Did she dare hope whoever stood beyond the edges of her fear might help them?

Slowly the shawl moved from above Sariah and Hannah. Sariah clutched Hannah even tighter and began to beg. Hannah stirred from her sleep.

"Please, do not hurt my daughter," Sariah pleaded. She opened her eyes and squinted up at the sunlight and the men who stood over the wagon. Their faces were dark from the sun but clean. Their eyes were gentle.

"No one will hurt you," the man named John said. "You are among friends."

A skin of water was handed to him, and he passed it to Sariah.

"Here, drink," he said.

She pushed herself up awkwardly, her heart still pounding, and accepted the water with shaky hands.

"First, my daughter," she said. She turned to Hannah, who was awake and looking calmly up at the men. Holding Hannah's head up as best she could, Sariah dribbled water into Hannah's mouth, then drank herself. After wiping her mouth with the back of her bloody hands, she handed the water back.

"Thank you," she said humbly, refusing to look at his eyes, embarrassed at her need. Her heart began to beat slower.

"What brings you to this lonely place?" another man with a quiet voice asked.

Pulling herself up by the side of the wagon, she could see even more men behind the ones by the wagon. They all looked at her with compassion. She felt a tiny spark of hope in her heart.

"My daughter is palsied," she said with a quivering voice. "We have traveled a long way, and robbers took all that we had."

"Please, let us help you," John said. "You are safe."

Strong hands reached for her and lifted her down. She initially drew back from them, but, without willing it, her fear was replaced with a calmness that seemed curious to her, and she let them help her out of the wagon. Hannah continued to lie quietly, staring with wide, deep eyes.

When Sariah finally stood beside the wagon, she pulled her dirty clothes around to regain some part of her dignity. She drew her matted hair back from her face and dared to look up. The men parted before her. There in front of her stood the man who looked the kindest of all. Although his clothes were also brown and humble, they seemed white compared to the others. She stopped and lifted her eyes up to him. There was something familiar about him, but she didn't recall ever meeting him before.

Then, a recognition began as a warmth in her heart and spread throughout her body, filling every fiber of her being with the comfort of a long-ago star. Her whole universe suddenly shrunk to see only the man before her. The shrieks of the birds became melodies, and the brown hills grew greener. No thoughts of Hannah being harmed burdened her soul.

He held his hand out, as his dark eyes pierced her soul and drew out the pain of so many years to replace it with peace. She was unable to look away. Her world was only him.

"Why are you traveling so far from any village?" he asked. His voice was at the same time stronger than any she had ever heard, yet as mild as a mother's reassurances.

"I . . . I am seeking the savior," she said, lowering her eyes and putting her hand in his.

Then, at his touch, she knew she had found him and raised her eyes to his. He smiled at her, and joy flowed into her soul.

"You are the savior," she whispered. She raised up to stand

tall in her testimony, weak with excitement at the ending of her journey, yet stronger than she had ever felt.

"Your faith is strong, my daughter," he said evenly. His voice was the warmth of the star, once forgotten, now familiar, shining through her window so long ago.

She sank to her knees and for the first time in many years, the tears that escaped her eyes were tears of happiness. She looked up at him. In his eyes, she saw love and peace and all that she had ever hoped he would be, all that she had sought.

"What do you seek?" he asked.

"My daughter," she said quietly. "Will you heal my daughter?" She bowed her head again. "I have nothing to give. The robbers stole my necklace and my coins I brought. I have nothing. But will you have mercy on me and heal my Hannah?" Looking up, she pleaded with her eyes.

"I have no need of coins and jewels," he said. "Your faith is sufficient. Come." He held out his hand again and lifted her up.

From someplace inside her, she knew she was walking, but she could not feel her feet on the ground. They no longer hurt. Every step she took brought light that coursed through her body, seeking out and healing the anguish of her many years.

The men parted again in silence as he led her to the wagon where Hannah lay, twisted and bent, her mouth glistening with drool and grimacing in discomfort.

Reaching over the side, the Savior took Hannah's bent hand.

"Your mother's faith has made you well," he said calmly to Hannah. "Be healed."

Sariah watched in amazement, although it seemed familiar, as if she had seen what unfolded before her at a previous time, either in her prayers or another place in eternity. Could it be that healing Hannah was as simple as his saying so?

Before her, Hannah's hands and arms straightened out, her fingers wiggling and stretching. Her tight legs grew straight and filled with sinew and flesh. Her mouth relaxed, and she swallowed. The pale hollows of her cheekbones became rounded. She closed her eyes, a sublime look on her face. When she opened them, she was whole.

It took only a moment, or was it an eternity? Sariah did not know because time seemed to suspend itself at that place in the quiet wilderness.

The Savior pulled gently on Hannah's hand, and she easily sat up, bringing her hands before her, then feeling her face, her hair, her ears.

Sariah cried out in joy, unable to take her eyes off her daughter.

She held her hands out, and Hannah reached out to touch them.

"Mother," Hannah said clearly. "My mother." Tears filled her eyes and overflowed onto her cheeks.

The men stepped up to help Hannah from the wagon as if a miracle had not happened and Hannah had always been able to arise and climb down. Sariah turned and dropped once more to her knees in front of the Savior.

"Thank you, my Lord," she said over and over, her tears wetting his feet.

Once more he held out his hand and drew her up.

"Behold your daughter," he said.

Sariah turned and saw Hannah walking, straight and tall, toward her. She was beautiful and whole, her long shiny hair falling down around her shoulders. Her face shone. Hannah opened her arms, and Sariah fell into them.

They embraced, pulling back to stare at each other, to laugh and then to cry, then embraced again. Releasing her mother, Hannah easily knelt at the feet of the Savior.

"Thank you," she said, over and over, until he said, "Arise, Hannah. Return to your home and care for your mother."

The men brought the donkey back from where it had been nibbling leaves nearby and put it at the wagon. While Hannah and Sariah rejoiced and touched each other's faces, arms, and hands over and over, the men merely smiled at their joy as if they saw such healings taking place every day in their lives.

The Savior instructed two men to travel with Sariah and Hannah home and two others to find a donkey for him.

Hannah and Sariah climbed onto the wagon bench, Sariah's feet now also healed, as two men led the wagon onto the road. Her arm around her daughter, who sat close beside her, Sariah turned and watched the Savior until they disappeared over the hill and she could no longer see him.

They traveled home, hands clasped, rejoicing and speaking of all that had happened.

Epilogue

In the years to come, Hannah ministered to her mother as her mother had ministered to her for so long. Her hands, unused for a lifetime, proved nimble with the needle, and she and Sariah sat at their door sewing and relating their experience to all who would listen. As Sariah's eyes grew weaker, Hannah gradually took over the sewing for the people who came, and Sariah sat quietly beside her, often reaching over and touching her arm or her hair.

The people of their village never tired of hearing the wonderful story of the day when Sariah and Hannah, followed by two kind men, had walked into the village. Most did not recognize Hannah at first, but then, with cries of joy, they marveled at what had happened, touching her hands and her arms and throwing their own arms into the air with joy as she spoke to them.

Before they returned to their house, Sariah and Hannah stopped at Joanna's house, Hannah standing behind Sariah at the door. When Joanna first opened the door and saw it was Sariah, she cried with joy that she was all right, for she had gone to Sariah's house that day and found them gone. Then as she began chiding her for leaving, she saw the woman standing behind her friend, and her eyes grew wide.

Sariah stepped aside and quietly said, "I found the Savior, and he healed Hannah."

The rejoicing in their home lasted until evening when, tired from their long day, Sariah and Hannah walked to theirs.

Within days of their return home, when news of the Savior's cruel death reached the village, there was sadness to all who had come to believe in his miracles, but when Sariah and Hannah heard the tales that he walked the earth again after being dead for three days, they believed.

A widower named Gabriel, who came from another village to work at the blacksmith shop where Joshua had worked years before, walked down to Sariah and Hannah's home one day to meet the woman whose story he had heard. While Hannah calmly finished the hem of a dress, Sariah told him of her years of caring for Hannah, how much her daughter had suffered, and of the day she was healed. He said little, but glanced over at Hannah often during the story with a quiet smile.

Throughout the next months, he came often, bringing fruit and trinkets from the market and visiting with the women, entertaining them with his stories and jokes. Soon he came in the evenings and asked them to walk with him, but Sariah walked only as far as Joanna's house where she sat in the coolness and waited for Hannah and Gabriel to return.

"What do you remember of those many years?" he asked Hannah one day on their walk. They had stopped at Joshua's gravesite.

She looked down at the flower he had picked for her, then back up at him, a thoughtful expression twisting her lips slightly.

"I remember no pain," she said, "although my mother tells me I suffered. I remember the sounds of her lullabies, her gentle hands, and the smiling face and joyous laugh of my father. I remember being in my bed and feeling safe and warm because I knew my mother and father loved me."

Gabriel took one of her hands from her lap and turned it over to trace its lines with his finger.

She sighed and continued. "It is as if my life began when the savior took my hand," she said. "But when I look at the stars at night, it is as if I have always been well."

Smiling, she put her hand over his. "I just feel whole, but I can't really remember the pain of being broken."

After a few months of quiet, happy courtship, Gabriel and Hannah married and took Sariah into his larger home where her days were gentle. In the continuing miracle of her life, Hannah was blessed with a baby boy who looked like Joshua with dark, sparkling eyes and curly dark hair. They named him after Joshua, and he proved to be the delight of Sariah's life. She was content to spend hours watching him as he babbled and clapped his hands in joy at whatever came into his sight. When he learned to walk, she hobbled along beside him for hours with him holding tightly to her finger.

He was eight when he first heard the story of his mother and her healing as he leaned into his grandmother's lap one night after supper. His little head was cocked as he listened to the whole tale without saying a word.

When she was finished, he looked up at her and wiped away her tears with one chubby little finger. Then he wordlessly wrapped his arms around her in a hug. "Thank you for making my mother well," he said quietly into her shoulder.

165

About two years later, Sariah died in her sleep, and they buried her beside her Joshua.

Hannah often walked to her mother's grave, with Joshua and Gabriel, but many times alone after dinner. She could not mourn because in her heart she knew that her mother and father were together and she would join them one day.

Each visit ended with her kneeling before their graves and thanking her mother again for her faith that had blessed her life many times over. Rising up, she would look at the stars and smile. She wasn't sure, but she always thought there were two that sparkled brighter than the rest.

Discussion Questions

1. What can a reader of *Miracle of the Christmas Star* learn about faith, endurance, and patience?
2. As a reader, were you disappointed as Sariah's faith sometimes stumbled?
3. What similar experiences have you had in your life that tried your faith? How was your faith strengthened after such experiences?
4. How did God provide for Sariah and Hannah, even as he required her to wait for many years to see the fulfillment of her faith and hope?
5. Why do you think it was necessary for Sariah to lose everything she held dear before she received the miracle?
6. Discuss the underlying motif of stars throughout the book. What did stars symbolize? How did such symbolism add to the appeal and message of the book?
7. How did the various people in the novel react to Hannah's

handicap and why did they react as they did? If Sariah were your neighbor back in those times, how would you have responded to her struggles?

8. In what ways would you like to be more like Sariah?

About the Author

Susan Dean Elzey grew up as an Army brat, living all over the world, but found her home in Danville, Virginia, when she was fifteen. Soon after, she fell in love with poetry and writing. She raised seven children, her oldest daughter handicapped with cerebral palsy, which influences every moment of her life. Returning to school after seventeen years as a stay-at-home mom, she earned a degree in English and journalism and then a master's degree in literature. Along the way, she published three LDS novels.

In a blended family, Susan and her husband David have nine children and, so far, fourteen grandchildren. She works as a freelance writer and reporter in beautiful southern Virginia.

Susan has previously published *You're a Rock, Sister Lewis* with Hatrack River Publications; *True Rings the Heart* with Deseret Book; and *A Chance for Sarah* with Cedar Fort.

You may visit Susan online at www.susanelzey.com.